"I never did g   " Heinrick said, his eyes ahead.

Lilly fought a w   , yet her own objections e   reigner, the enemy. But a   only the crunch of prairie grass and the beating of her heart, she knew that wasn't a fair assessment. He deserved courtesy, if not her friendship. "Lillian," she whispered. "But my friends call me Lilly."

"Lilly it is, then." She saw a smile tug at his lips.

They walked through the velvet darkness, the field grass crunching under their steps, the crickets singing from the riverbed not far off, and a lazy ballad humming over the bluffs from distant campfires. The wind skimmed the aroma from a pot of stew and carried it across the prairie. Lilly's stomach flopped, but not from hunger.

"I guess I owe you." She peeked at Heinrick and saw his smile widen.

"How's that?"

"You're one up on me. You saved Frankie and now me."

Heinrick chuckled, and Lilly was oddly delighted.

"Well, let me see. How can you save me?"

SUSAN MAY WARREN and her family live in Northern Minnesota, a recent move after spending eight years in Far East Russia as missionaries. Although she grew up in Minnesota, she spent every summer in Mobridge, South Dakota, attending the Independence Day Rodeo and swimming in the Missouri River. With a B.A. in Communications from the University of MN, Susan May Warren is a multi-published author of both novellas and full-length Christian fiction. Find out more about Susan and her books at www.susanmaywarren.com.

Letters from the Enemy

Susan May Warren

Heartsong Presents

To Pops and Grandma Niedringhaus.
In my fondest recollections, I can see you sitting on the sofa,
still holding hands after three decades of marriage.
I miss you.
To Curt and MaryAnn Lund.
It's your memories that make my own so sweet.
To the Lord Jesus Christ, for loving me first.
Thank you for setting me free.

A note from the Author:
I love to hear from my readers! You may correspond with me
by writing:

Susan May Warren
Author Relations
PO Box 719
Uhrichsville, OH 44683

ISBN 1-59310-063-9

LETTERS FROM THE ENEMY

Our mission is to publish and distribute inspirational products offering
exceptional value and biblical encouragement to the masses.

All Scripture quotations are taken from the King James Version of the
Bible.

All of the characters and events in this book are fictitious. Any resem-
blance to actual persons, living or dead, or to actual events is purely
coincidental.

PRINTED IN THE U.S.A.

one

June 1918

"We're going to miss the train!" Lilly Clark dashed across the South Dakota prairie, trampling a clump of goldenrod with her dusty boots. The withering grass shimmered under the noonday sun. A humid wind skipped off the Missouri River, and clawed at her straw hat. She clamped a hand over the back of her head and pumped her legs faster toward the crumbling knoll that overlooked the town of Mobridge. Her heart beat out a race against her feet; she could already hear the train thundering through the valley.

Behind her, Marjorie Pratt strained to keep up. "Wait. . .for . . .me," she gasped.

Lilly forced herself up the hill, gulping deep breaths. At the crest, she yanked off her hat and wiped her brow. Squinting in the sunlight, she scanned the horizon and spotted the iron snake threading its way between bluffs and farmhouses toward the Mobridge depot.

"Is. . .it. . .here?" Marjorie staggered to the top.

"Almost," Lilly replied. "We have to hurry."

Marjorie shed her calico bonnet and patted her brow with it. "Just. . .let . . .me rest." Shielding her eyes, she searched for the train.

"It's over there," Lilly said, pointing. Her other hand clutched a lavender envelope, tinged with a thin layer of dust. She scowled and blew on the envelope, assigning the soil to the greedy wind. For a brief second she regretted the extra moments it had taken to saturate the precious letter in perfume and dry it, but the thought of Reggie's smile as he smelled the fresh lilac erased her doubts. She would just have to run faster.

She cast a look at her friend. Marjorie fanned herself, breathing heavily.

"Give me your letter, and I'll go on ahead," Lilly suggested.

Marjorie shook her head. "No. . .I'll make it."

Lilly nodded, then scrambled down the cliff, stepping on roots and boulders to slow her descent. There was an easier way into town, but taking that route would sacrifice valuable minutes and probably her delivery of this week's letter. She heard Marjorie hiss as she started down the cliff behind her, but Lilly knew her friend would make it. Marjorie came from sturdy English stock. She just didn't have the exercise of hoeing and weeding the kitchen garden in her favor. Instead, Marjorie devoted all her time to Red Cross work, assembling field kits.

"I'm going to fall!" Marjorie shrieked, sounding more angry than afraid. "It's your fault we're late! If we'd left on time, we wouldn't have had to scramble across the prairie like a couple of jackrabbits!"

Lilly laughed. "You're hardly a jackrabbit, Marj. Just be careful!" With Lilly's long brown hair quickly unfurling in the wind and her tanned face, she knew she was much more likely to be compared to a longhaired wild animal than her dainty friend. Thankfully, Reggie didn't seem to care that she didn't have Marjorie's sweetheart face, candy red lips, and blond hair.

Lilly reached flat land and sped toward town, picking up as much speed as her narrow gingham skirt would allow. At least it was wider than the dreadful hobble skirts that had been in fashion before the war. She'd ripped out two before her mother conceded defeat and allowed Lilly to sew her own styles.

The train's whistle let out an explosive shrill. Lilly glanced back at her friend, now a good fifty feet behind her.

"Lilly, hurry!" Marjorie waved her on.

Squinting into the sun, Lilly spotted the tiny depot, situated on the edge of town like a like a lighthouse to the outlying northern farms. As the train pulled in and belched black exhaust, Lilly ignored the fire in her lungs and forced her legs to move.

The exhaust settled, and Lilly caught sight of the doors of two livestock boxcars being opened and a ramp being propped up to each entry. Cowboys ascended the ramps, disappeared into the black hole of the boxcars, and emerged dragging angry bulls or frightened horses.

Suddenly, a scab of sagebrush caught the edge of her boot. Lilly screeched, stumbled, and directed her attention back to the jagged prairie.

The train whistle blared, emitting its first departure signal, and fear stabbed at Lilly's heart. She leaped over a railroad tie, used as a property divider and, grinning between gasps, glued her eyes to the station's platform steps.

If she'd been one step closer, Lilly would have been crushed under the hooves of a mustang, dancing in a frenzied escape from his handler He blew by her like a tornado, his whiplike tail lashing her face and neck. Lilly screamed, stumbled, and plowed headfirst into the dirt, swallowing a mouthful of prairie in her vanished grin.

She sprawled there dazed, hurt, and dirty.

"Are you all right, *Fraulein?*"

The words barely registered in her fog of confusion. Then a strong arm hooked her waist, pulling her to her feet. Lilly absently held on as she steadied herself. She ached everywhere, but nowhere more than in her pride.

"*Fraulein*, are you hurt?"

She looked up and gaped at a Nordic giant in a cream-colored ten-gallon cowboy hat. Dirt smudged his tanned face and dark sapphire eyes radiated concern under a furrowed brow.

"Sorry. That stallion is a rascal."

Lilly ran her trembling hand over her mouth, trying to gather in her scattered wits while she took in the man's apologetic smile. Her disobedient heart continued to gallop a rhythm of terror.

The cowboy squinted at her, as if assessing her ability to stand on her own, and Lilly realized she still clutched his muscled arm. She yanked her hand away, a blush streaming up her cheeks. When he bent over, she noticed how his curly blond hair scuffed the back of his red cotton shirt collar.

"This yours?" He held the lavender envelope, now dirty and crumpled between two grimy fingers.

"Oh!" Lilly cried in dismay. She reached for it, but the cowboy untied his handkerchief from his neck and used it to clean the envelope before handing it over.

Tears pricked Lilly's eyes. Her letter to Reggie, ruined. "Thank you," she whispered.

"Sorry," the cowboy muttered.

The train whistle screamed again. Lilly jumped, remembering her mission. She turned toward the depot but pain bunched at her ankle and shot up her leg. She cried out and began to crumple.

The cowboy gripped her elbow, steadying her. "You are hurt."

"Well, I would think so, after being almost run over by your horse," Lilly snapped, unable to hide her irritation.

"Can I help you inside?"

Lilly shook her head. "I can make it. Just go get that beast before it kills somebody." She yanked her elbow from his grasp and turned on her heel, biting her lip against the pain.

"I really am sorry," he offered again.

Ignoring the last apology, Lilly hobbled to the platform stairs and gripped the railing. She paused, then glanced over her shoulder at him.

The cowboy had taken off his hat and was crunching it in his hands. He gazed at her with eyes steeped in remorse. Her anger melted slightly. "Just go get that horse, Sir. I'll be fine."

He nodded and shoved his hat on his head. Lilly blew out a frustrated breath and climbed the stairs, wincing. Reaching the top, she swept up wisps of her tangled hair and tucked them under her straw hat. She felt flushed and grimy, but at that moment she didn't care who saw her. Her letter had to make the mail train.

Lilly limped across the platform and entered the depot. The screen door squealed on its hinges. Two men looked up and stared at her.

She ignored the first, a grizzled Native American perched on a lonely bench by the window, and approached the second, a tall, pinched man who eyed her sternly.

"Hello, Mr. Carlson," Lilly said, noting her shaky voice and smiling. He took in her appearance and flared an eyebrow.

"Do you have some mail to send to France?"

Lilly held out the lavender envelope. He grabbed it and dropped it in a bulging canvas bag.

"Just in time." He bent to tie the bag.

"Wait, please." Lilly peered out the window, searching for Marjorie, just now hauling herself up the platform steps.

Mr. Carlson scowled. "Hurry up."

Lilly gave the station manager a pleading smile. "Please, it's for true love's sake."

Mr. Carlson sighed and shook his head. "This war has generated more true love. . ."

He waited, however, until Marjorie trudged through the door and handed him her own bulging envelope, before closing the bag and dragging it out to the hissing train.

Marjorie and Lilly watched in silence as the porters loaded the mailbag, hoping the letters would, indeed, find their recipients. Lilly realized it was a fragile link, this postal system across the Atlantic. She only hoped it was strong enough to sustain the covenant of love between her and Reggie Larsen.

Mr. Carlson returned, his brow dripping with perspiration. He leaned upon the tall stool behind his counter, glowering at the two girls. "So, what are ya waiting for?"

Lilly eyed him warily. "You don't suppose there is any chance you could look. . ."

"Be gone with ya!" Carlson bellowed, reaching for a glass of tepid water languishing next to his schedule book. "You'll get the mail in your boxes, like always."

Marjorie put a hand on Lilly's arm. "Let's go get a lemonade."

As they exited the depot, Marjorie noticed Lilly's limp. "What happened to you?" She stepped back and surveyed her friend. "Why, you're filthy!"

Lilly brushed herself off. "A wild mustang plowed me over."

Marjorie slid a hand around Lilly's waist. "Are you going to be all right?"

Lilly smiled wanly and nodded. Her ankle would be fine. What upset her more was the lingering image of a handsome young cowboy who had nearly derailed her well-laid plans.

two

"Can we. . . rest. . .?" Lilly braced her arm on Marjorie's shoulder and gritted her teeth against the pain spearing her leg.

"You're really hurt, Lilly," Marjorie said. "Maybe I should take you home. I could ask Willard if he would drive you in his Packard."

"No!" Lilly snapped, then regretted her tone. "I want to wait for Reggie's letter. I haven't heard from him in two weeks."

Marjorie gave her a sympathetic smile. "Don't worry. I'm sure he's fine."

Fine? Lilly stamped down her bitterness, but it sprang back like a hardy thistle. Fine would be him here, planning their wedding, preparing to be a pastor. Fine would be him riding roundup or walking her home from church on Sundays. Fine had nothing to do with war or Germans or the fear that boiled in her chest.

She knew the truth. She read the newspapers, despite her father's ministrations to hide them, and knew how "fine" the doughboys were in France. Some were coming home with limbs missing, others in pine boxes. She bit her lip to ward off tears. How fine would she be if Reggie returned home in a flag-draped coffin? Then whom would she marry? Lilly winced at her selfish thought and shook her head to dismiss it.

A heated wind snared a strand of hair from her bun and sent it dancing about her face. Lilly caught it and wiped it back. "Yes, he'll be fine," she agreed, needing to hear the affirmation.

"You should be happy Reggie proposed before he left." Marjorie untied her bonnet and wiped the back of her neck.

How did Marjorie always manage to look beautiful, even under the blistering prairie heat? Her buttery hair turned

11

golden in the blinding sun, and her creamy face never burned. Try as she might, Lilly couldn't control the mass of freckles that overran her face each summer; and her hair, well, she'd seen a prettier mane on her father's worn-out plow horse.

"He didn't formally propose, Marj." Lilly rotated her throbbing ankle, longing to unlace her high boots. "He just kissed me and told me we'd be married when he returned."

Marj sighed. "But that's enough." Her eyes glistened. "Harley didn't even do that much. Just waved with his floppy army cap as the train rolled out of the station."

Lilly smirked. "That's just because he refused to stand in line with all the other boys saying good-bye to the town sweetheart."

Marjorie blushed and had the decency to look chagrined. "If I had half as many suitors as you—"

"You didn't need them. You have the most eligible bachelor of them all." Marjorie's eyes twinkled, and Lilly was instantly grateful for a friend who didn't point out the stark reality. Even when Reggie had been away at seminary and the town teeming with cowboys and railroad brakemen, not one had taken a shine to the poor Clark girl from the farm up the road.

Then Reggie reappeared on her front porch. Fresh out of seminary, he told her that life with him would be heaven and that he'd been waiting for her since she was in pigtails. His wide smile was like honey to her heart. He'd changed, of course, become refined, serious, exacting of himself and others, but that only inspired her respect. He never stepped over the line with her and treated her as if she was his own cherished possession. Reggie was her future, her security, the man God had chosen for her. Her feelings felt more along the lines of gratefulness, but then again, who wouldn't be grateful for the security of a husband and a family? Wasn't gratefulness a part of love? Reggie would protect her and give her a home. Reggie was God's steadfast reminder He had not forgotten her. After all the years of obeying the church and her parents and striving to be a woman of God, the good Lord had finally noticed and sent her Reggie.

And, if she did everything right, he would be hers forever.

"Let's go," Lilly said, pointing her gaze toward town. "Please drag me to Miller's, Marjie. If I don't get a lemonade soon, I might perish."

Marjorie laughed and shouldered Lilly's weight. They hobbled down the dusty road toward Mobridge.

They passed the shanties the Milwaukee Road had built for their brakemen and engineers who worked this end of the line and turned the corner onto Main Street.

"Billy Harper, you watch it!" Marjorie cried as a large hoop rolled in their direction. The barefoot ten year old deftly turned it, and a wide grin shone on his dusty face. As they shuffled along the boardwalks that edged the handful of false-front buildings, they dodged women in wilted bonnets scurrying from shop to shop, baskets of produce in one hand and unruly toddlers in the other. The clop of horses' hooves echoed on the hard-packed street.

Lilly spied Clive Torgesen parked in front of the armory, propped against his gleaming Model T, arms folded over his chest as he accepted the fawning of goggle-eyed teenage boys admiring his new toy. Clive spotted her and pulled a greeting on his black Stetson. Lilly turned away, not wanting to give the town troublemaker any encouragement.

The smell of baking bread drifted from Ernestine's Fresh Food Market, delicious enough to tempt Lilly to change her destination, but her parched throat won. She and Marjorie shuffled into Miller's Cafe.

Ed Miller had his hands full serving a row of thirsty cow-boys and field hands who were downing lemonade or sipping coffee. Marjorie joined the line by the cashier as Lilly claimed a spot by the bookshelf near the windowsill. The shelf sported a yellowing pile of magazines from the East: *Vanity Fair, Ladies Home Journal,* and a thick stack of *American Railroad* journals. Lilly picked up a week-old *Milwaukee Journal,* flipped through it, and listened to the murmur of muddled conversation around her. Opinions of Wilson's latest political blunders, General Pershing's field maneuvers, skirmishes on the western front, and Hoover's wartime food regulations seemed to be the talk of the day.

"They're movin' the draft up ta age forty-five, I hear," said a weathered cowpoke.

"It don' matter, I'm gonna enlist anyway," replied his neighbor. "At least then we'll get ta eat some of the beef we've been tendin'. These ration days are gonna whittle me down ta bones."

"Yeah, but it might be better than having to face those Germans with nothin' more than a spear at the enda your gun. I hear Pershing has 'em runnin' straight into gunfire with no more than a yelp and a prayer."

"That ain't true, Ollie. I know that our doughboys have themselves real live ma-chan-i-cal rifles. Spit out bullets faster than rain from a black sky. I do think I'd like to get my hands on one a those."

"Well, you're gonna have to live through the boat ride across the ocean first. I heard Ed Miller's boy left a trail from New York to Paris."

Lilly smiled as she heard the cowboys' guffaw and Ed's growl in their direction. She wondered what the war really looked like, up close.

Marjorie nudged her, holding a fresh glass of lemonade.

"Thanks." Lilly took the cold drink and held it to her face, letting the cool glass refresh her skin. Then, she gulped it half down. Marjorie's shocked face stopped her from tilting it bottoms up.

"Sorry." Lilly licked her lips. "I was thirsty."

Marjorie scowled. "So it seems."

Lilly cringed, but caught sight of Rev. Larsen emerging from the alley between Ernestine's and Morrie's Barbershop. Lilly shoved her almost-empty drink into her friend's hand. "I'll meet you at the postal." She hopped toward the door, ignoring Marjorie's cry of protest.

Lilly limped across the street, dodging shouts of outrage

from two cowboys on horseback and upsetting Billy Harper's hoop. "Rev. Larsen, Sir!"

Rev. Larsen halted two paces from Morrie's front entrance. His angular face held no humor as he surveyed her disheveled appearance. "Lilly, what happened to you?"

Startled, she stared down at her dress. Grime embedded its folds and the sudden image of a cowboy with jeweled blue eyes glinting apology scattered her thoughts. Her mouth hung open, wordless.

"You ought to take better care of your appearance." Rev. Larsen's voice snapped her back to reality. "Just because Reggie is halfway around the world doesn't mean he doesn't care how you look. You have his reputation to uphold now." He cocked a spiny eyebrow.

Lilly bit back defensiveness and instead extracted a respectful tone. "Have you heard from Reggie?"

"Of course not. He has a war to fight. You just do your part and keep writing to him. I am sure he will write back when he can." He stabbed a skeletal finger into the air. "We all have a job to do in this great war, Lilly, and yours is to make sure our Reggie remembers what he has to come home to."

Lilly blew out a trickle of frustrated breath. "I have been writing, Sir."

Rev. Larsen laid his bony hand on her shoulder, his gray eyes softening. "I'm sure you have. Mail's often slow at the front. Be patient and trust him to the Lord's hands. He'll write soon."

Lilly nodded. Rev. Larsen stepped into the barbershop, but his parting words lingered. Reggie was in God's hands, and God wouldn't let her down. She, her family, even the entire town knew she would become Mrs. Reginald Larsen, and she would trust the Lord to make it so. The alternative was simply unthinkable. Besides, she'd been so faithful to God, done everything right. She deserved God's cooperation, didn't she?

"Have you lost your senses?"

Lilly whirled and met a frowning Marjorie. "You look like

you've wrestled a tornado, and you run up to Rev. Larsen like a lost puppy? What's he going to think about his son's fiancée?" Marjorie scowled. "You've got to learn to curb your recklessness if you're going to be a pastor's wife."

Lilly grimaced. Impulsiveness was her worst trait, constantly running before her to embroil her in a stew of awkward situations. If she weren't careful, Reggie would choose someone else to mother his flock.

"C'mon, let's check the mail." Marjorie tugged on Lilly's arm.

At the post office, they crowded in behind anxious women waiting for the mail.

"Is it here?" Marjorie whispered.

Lilly shrugged, but her heart skipped wildly. A letter from Reggie—something to remind her she was still his. *Please, O Lord.* Then she glimpsed Mrs. Tucker as the thin woman pushed through the crowd. She held a letter in her hands, raised high as if a trophy. Lilly's heart gave a loud inward cry, and Marjorie breathed the answer, "It's here."

Although the line moved faster than expected, an eternity passed before Lilly finally stood at the counter, biting her lower lip as they checked the Donald Clark family box.

They brought her a letter, postmarked from France, with tightly scrawled handwriting that could only belong to Reggie. Lilly clutched it to her chest and pushed her way to the door.

On the dusty street, Lilly paused, fighting the impulse to tear open Reggie's letter and know in seconds whether he was all right, unhurt, and missing her. But then it would be over, the news spilled out like sand on the Missouri River shore. Lilly gulped a breath and calmed her heart. No, it was better to wait, to savor each word and hear his voice as she read the letter slowly under the oak tree behind her house. Or perhaps she would go to the ridge, past the grove of maples that overlooked the river, and imagine him beside her as the sun slipped over to his side of the world. Lilly tucked the letter into her skirt pocket.

Marjorie's scream of delight preceded her from the post

office. "It's from Harley!" She waved a wrinkled envelope at Lilly, her smile streaming across her face.

She ripped open her letter, and the envelope drifted to the ground. Lilly picked it up, watching Marjorie silently mouth Harley's words.

"He's okay," Marjorie mumbled absently.

Lilly breathed relief and gazed westward at the sun, now a jagged orange ball, low on the horizon. It had lost its fervor during the downward slide, and the air carried on it the cool scent of the Missouri. The field locusts began their twilight buzz, beckoning her homeward. Lilly limped away, leaving her friend standing in the street, a pebble among a beach of other women: sweethearts, mothers, and daughters who had paused to read the mail. But not just any mail. . .mail from France, Belgium, and all along the Western Allied front lines. Mail that gave them one more day to hope the madness and worry would soon end.

Reggie's letter burned a hole in Lilly's pocket, beseeching her to open it. She put her hand on the envelope, thankful for its presence. It was a shield against the unrelenting reminder of war and the horror that threatened to crash down upon her if Reggie never came home.

three

The handwriting was bold and sturdy, the very essence of Reggie. Lilly clearly pictured him: his long fingers gripping a stubby pencil as he bent over the parchment, a shock of black hair flung over his chestnut brown eyes.

Lilly caught herself. Reggie's black hair had been shaved, kept short to ward off lice. And, the paper was smudged. Reality stabbed at her. Reggie would never willingly send her anything less than perfect. Her brow knit in worry as she devoured his words.

My Dearest Lilly,

  I would like to tell you it's quiet here, that Europe is beautiful and I'll return soon, but I know how you hate lies, and those would be falsehoods of great proportion. In truth, I sit now in a support trench, my back against a muddy dugout wall, hoping Harley and Chuck will help me stay warm tonight. It's not that it's cold; on the contrary, the blistering heat of June has been my greatest challenge yet. The urge to throw off my pack, my helmet, and this grating ammunition belt and scratch the sweat and slime from my body is nearly as great as my desire to gaze into your emerald eyes and see that you miss me, desperately, I hope. No, I'm not referring to the cold that comes with a gathering Dakota blizzard. I mean the cold fear that lurks in the silence between offensives. Alone, I cannot staunch l the panic that floods my heart when I hear the command, "Over the top!" The charges are bloody and hopeless. We fling ourselves headlong toward the Germans, hoping to win their trench and thereby regain Europe, yard by yard. But I will never erase the sight of so many fellow soldiers, pale and lifeless in the mist at dawn, tangled in the lines of barbed wire that run through the no-man's-land between enemy lines. I stare at them and wonder if and when that will be me. It is then I shiver.

But Harley and Chuck help fend off the cold. Together we remember the things worth living for: you and Marjorie, little Christian and Olive and all the others we protect. We are our own fighting unit, and these brothers have become closer to me than blood. It is with them I hope to return to you, soon.

Our troops are spread throughout Europe, providing the gaps left by Allied casualties in the French and British lines. I cannot tell you where I am stationed, but I serve with men such as Frances, Marc-Luc, Kenneth, and Simon.

As I reread this letter, I realize it's seems hopeless . But I am not hopeless. I have you and the vivid memory of your brown hair loosened and fingered by the wind as you waved me off that day, not quite a year ago, as our train pulled away from the platform. Your tears etched sorrow down your cheeks and spoke to me of your devotion to our plans. My thoughts are ever turned toward you, and if (I hate to write it, but I must) I should fall and perish on foreign soil, I pray you will remember me as yours, devoted until the end.

Faithfully,
Reggie

Lilly hugged the letter. Despite the horrors of war, the fear he fought by the hour, and the evident ache of loneliness, Reggie remained the perfect gentleman, honorable and devoted. Tears filled her eyes. Oh! God would just have to bring him back.

Lilly read the letter again, her tears blurring every word as night enfolded her. Lilly listened to the crickets hum and the melody of the grass as the breeze danced off the river. She wondered if Reggie was warm now. She ached to do something for him. . .but she could do nothing but pray. Reggie was in God's hands.

Wasn't that, however, what she feared the most? God was so unpredictable. What if Reggie wasn't a part of her future? What if he was to die in the war and she would never marry the boy she'd waited so long for?

But surely, God wouldn't do that to His faithful servant. Surely, she'd earned the right for Reggie to come home safely. She'd done everything right and proper, acting in perfect obedience. Wasn't that what religion was all about?

Lilly ground her nails into the palms of her hands as she looked past the dark fields toward the sparkling stars. She would not let panic leak into her letters. It would only spoil the pledge she and Reggie had made. Of course, God wanted them together. He was good and loving and blessed those who followed the church's teaching.

God could prove His love, however, by bringing Reggie safely home.

She picked a blade of grass and freed it to the wind. Reggie belonged to her. They had plans, a God-given future, and nothing, not even a war, could destroy it.

❧

Grateful to be out of the house, Lilly tightened her grip on her grocery basket's handle and picked up her pace along the dirt road. The heat pushed everyone to the edge of composure. It slithered into the house from the fields, soiling cotton blouses and melting patience. With three wild younger siblings, her sister Olive and her baby Christian living under the Clark roof, Lilly jumped at the scorching two-mile trek into town, hoping to find reprieve for her frazzled nerves.

Now, only the drone of buzzing grasshoppers accompanied her on the journey into Mobridge.

Daughters sent on last-minute errands packed Ernestine's Fresh Food Market . Lilly weaved past barrels of dill pickles, jars of sauerkraut, and burlap bags of dried corn and buckwheat kernels. The heady scent of peppermint and coffee encircled her as she slid into line, greeting Marjorie's sister Evelyn.

"What do you need today, Lilly?" Ernestine sighed, the

sheen of perspiration glistening on her wide brow.

"Two pounds of flour, please."

Willard, Ernestine's balding husband, winked at Lilly as Ernestine dipped out the flour and poured it into Lilly's canvas bag.

"Get any letters from the front?" Willard's voice stayed low, but laughter sang in his eyes.

"Maybe," she replied, blushing.

His gray eyes twinkled. He winked again and turned away. Ernestine handed her the flour, and Lilly dropped a nickel into the shopkeeper's sweaty palm.

The basket groaned as Lilly dropped the bag of flour into it. She tucked it into the crook of her arm and pushed toward the door, where the late afternoon sun flooded over the threshold. As Lilly stepped out of the shop, it blinded her, and she plowed straight into a pair of thick, muscled arms.

"Oh, excuse me!" Lilly stumbled backward.

Wide hands clamped on her upper arms to steady her. Her victim's tall frame blocked the sun, and Lilly stared unblinking at a Viking with a crooked smile, golden blond hair, and eyes blue like the sky an hour before a prairie rainstorm. Lilly's heart thumped like a war drum in her chest.

"You again!" She pulled her arms from his grasp.

He fingered the brim of his battered ten-gallon hat in apology and salutation. "I keep running you over, *Fraulein.*" His grin teased, but his eyes spoke apology. "Pardon me."

Lilly felt a blush. "It's my fault this time." Her gaze skimmed his scuffed brown boots, then returned to his angular face. An attractive layer of blond whiskers outlined his rueful smile.

The cowboy's grin evaporated. For a moment, his brilliant blue eyes kneaded her with an obscure emotion. Then it morphed into pure mischievousness. He stepped aside and doffed his hat, sweeping low and indicating, like an Arthurian knight, that she should pass.

"Thank you," Lilly stammered. She swept past him, feeling his gaze on her back as she took off in a rapid clip

Lilly was passing Miller's when she heard the ruckus start. Angry voices and a string of curses punctuated the air. Lilly whirled, horrified, wondering who would use such vile language in the middle of Main Street.

Brad, Gordy, and Allen Craffey, three burly brakemen and recent imports from Milwaukee, surrounded the man Lilly had bumped into. They pushed him with their offensive words to the middle of the street.

"What's the matter, can't ya read?" Brad brandished a long stick, poking at his victim.

Lilly's stomach clenched. The cowboy had his hands outstretched, as if trying to explain. Gibberish spewed from his mouth.

"I said, can't ya read?" Brad taunted.

The cowboy stilled, but his words hung like a foul odor. A crowd began to gather. Lilly could smell suspicion in the sizzling breeze. Then she saw the foreigner ball his fists.

"See this. . .?" Gordy dashed up the steps to Ernestine's. An assembly of speechless women, Ernestine included, watched as he ripped a sign from her door. Lilly knew it well and hated it: "No Indians allowed."

Gordy scrambled down the steps and flung it at the man's feet. "No Injuns allowed!"

The stunned onlookers stared at him, awaiting his reply. The cowboy spoke in tight, clipped English, enunciating each word. "I. . .am. . .not. . .an. . .Indian."

Obviously. His fair skin and white blond hair could hardly be compared to the crimson tan of the Oglala Sioux. But his accent alienated him. Lilly swallowed the hard lump in her throat. What was this young, strong foreigner doing here when the majority of Mobridge's male population was overseas fighting for their lives? An ugly murmur shifted through the crowd.

Lilly noticed Ed Miller, Roy Flanner, and Morrie from the barbershop clumped on the boardwalk, watching with stony eyes.

"Where ya from, Blondie?" Brad said it, but it could have been anyone's voice.

"Deutschland." The cowboy lifted his chin slightly.

"Dutch land!" Gordy screamed. "Where's that?"

"I think it's near England!"

"It's next to Norway!"

"Isn't that where they make those wooden shoes?"

Lilly felt as if she'd been slugged. *No, it's our enemy, the people who are trying to kill your sons and husbands.* They had a German right here in their midst.

Brad took the confusion and turned it into violence. He cursed and shoved the German with his stick. Lilly held in a horrified scream as Gordy pounced on the German's back and Brad landed a blow into the man's chest. He sagged slightly, lost his hat. Brad trampled it and slammed his fist into the German's stomach. He grunted. Lilly winced. A broken bottle suddenly appeared in Allen's grip. The wiry Craffey sneered at the German and slashed wildly.

Lilly's breath caught when the German threw Gordy off his back then caught Brad's stick above his head. He wrenched it from Brad's grasp, while dodging Allen's jagged weapon.

Why didn't the German attack? Throw a punch to defend himself? Lilly teetered at the edge of the boardwalk, horrified yet transfixed. Craffeys came at him time and again, yet he stood his ground, no quarter given, but none taken.

Allen hurled the bottle at the German, and it ripped a gash down the side of his face.

Lilly bit her trembling lip and fought with herself. She should help him. No one had moved to his defense. Shame tasted like bile in her throat. What kind of town had Mobridge turned into when a group of Christians let a man be beaten? What had he done but be a foreigner in a suffering town?

Then again, he wasn't any foreigner; he was German. He deserved to be beaten.

Her sense of justice grabbed her and screamed logic. This

German was not part of the Central Powers, the German/Austrian force that started the Great War. He might be an unwelcome presence in their town—but he hadn't caused the deaths of their South Dakota cowboys.

And Lilly could not let the Craffey boys cause his death.

She dropped the basket and ran headlong into the fight.

four

Lilly didn't know what terrified her more, the venomous look on Gordy Craffey's face or her own bloodcurdling scream. The sound scattered the Craffey brothers with the effectiveness of three quick jabs.

Brad and Allen stared at her, eyes wide, backing away from her. Lilly halted in a strategic location between the Craffey brothers and the bleeding German. Balling her hands on her hips, she planted her feet and tried to appear fierce. Her pulse roared in her ears.

Gordy Craffey picked himself off the dirt. He stepped toward Lilly like a boxer, his fists high. "Get out of here, Lilly Clark."

Lilly shook her head, trying to summon her voice. She glanced at the German. His wide chest rose and fell in rapid rhythm; blood dripped off his chin.

"I said get, Lilly." Hatred animated Gordy's dark eyes.

Lilly held her breath. Would Gordy strike her? With his whitened fists and neck muscles bunched, he resembled a mad bull. Lilly battled the impulse to flee. *There are at least fifty people watching,* she reasoned. *Gordy wouldn't dare hit me.* Judging by the angry scowls from the onlookers, Lilly wasn't so sure they wouldn't join ranks with the Craffeys and drag her, kicking and screaming, from the fight.

She crossed her hands over her chest and fought a violent tremble. "Leave him alone, Gordy. Save your anger for the real enemy."

Apprehension rode through Mobridge on a smoldering breeze. Lilly smelled the foul odor of perspiration as she met Gordy's black eyes. They narrowed, raising gooseflesh over Lilly.

"Get him outta here," he growled.

Lilly freed a shuddering breath and glanced at the German. "Do you have a wagon?"

His gaze remained on Gordy as he jerked a nod.

"Good, you can drive me home."

Lilly dodged Gordy's searing gaze as she and the German back stepped. When they reached a graying buckboard parked in front of Bud Graham's pharmacy, the German untied the rig while Lilly scanned the faces of the townspeople. It wouldn't take long for news to race across the prairie. She briefly considered bandages for the German's wound, but when she saw the cold abhorrence in Bud's eyes, she snared her broken basket and climbed into the wagon.

"Where to?" the man asked without looking at her.

"North out of town, about two miles."

The acrid stares of the townspeople burned Lilly's neck as she rode tall and eyes forward on the bench. But her mind wrung out her impulsive actions. How many understood the German's words? Lilly bit a quivering lip.

They churned the dust into a thick cloud as they galloped out of the valley and into the yellowing bluffs. Horror throbbed behind Lilly's every thought, and only her grip on the bench kept her from covering her face with her hands and weeping. What had she just done?

Aside from the obvious foolishness of riding alone with a stranger, she'd just stuck her neck out, in full glare view of the entire Mobridge population, for a virtual enemy, for someone her own Reggie was trying to kill—and avoid being killed by! *Traitor.* Lilly went cold.

A mile out of town, the German slowed the horses to a walk. The road rippled as waves of heat skimmed it. Overhead, a stealthy red-tailed hawk hunted jackrabbits in an erratic pursuit. The field locusts hissed, interrupted only by the roar of an intermittent breeze. Perspiration layered Lilly's forehead and began a slow slide down her cheek.

She glanced at the man she'd saved. Blood continued to drip onto his work pants, but he seemed mindless of it. His eyes were trained upon the horses, the endless prairie, perhaps even a land far away across the ocean.

"Are you okay?" Lilly ventured. *No, obviously not!* Lilly grimaced at her question. *He is bleeding and was attacked by three men!* Lilly recalled the confusion, perhaps even panic, which twisted his foreign words. It had horrified her; now she only felt sorry for him. Her own countrymen sickened her.

Bigotry always incensed her. It only took her history with the never-ending problem of the prairie dogs to see that injustice eclipsed all rational thinking on her part. Her father was always inventing new ways to extinguish the pests, and it wasn't without a measure of sympathy for the furry creatures from the women in his family. For a time, Lilly headed up a smuggling ring, teaching Bonnie, DJ, and Frankie how to sleuth out and uncover the dammed-up dens. Then her father discovered their scheme and employed the thin end of a willow switch to help them see the error of their ways. Nevertheless, pity swept over Lilly every time she saw one dart through their carrot patch, and although she shooed them away, she still couldn't bring herself to alert the local posse. Perhaps, as Lilly watched the Craffey brothers pummel the hapless blond German, she'd been reminded of a prairie dog—hated and stalked. Perhaps that was why she flew into the middle of a street brawl, abandoning her common sense.

She was going to regret that act as soon as her father found out. And what if Reggie heard about it? Aiding and abetting the enemy in his own backyard. Lilly shuddered.

The horses snorted. Their coats were spotted with sweat, darkening their chocolate hides. The German clucked twice to them, encouraging their labors.

Out of the corner of her eye, Lilly scrutinized the blond, German cowboy. His eyes were hooded, and they squinted in the light. He'd left his hat in the dust back in Mobridge, and Lilly couldn't help notice his golden hair had dried into a curly, askew mop. He had a strong jaw, now clenched, as if reliving the fight.

Lilly cleared her throat and asked again, louder, "Are you okay?"

The German shrugged, deflecting her concern. Lilly frowned, annoyed. Didn't he know what her actions might cost her?

"You could at least thank me! You know, I'll never be welcome in town again because of you."

"I didn't ask for your help." His toneless reply sent fury into her veins.

"But you needed it. They could have killed you!"

The German turned, pinned on her an eternal, impenetrable gaze. Lilly raised her chin against it. Then the corner of his mouth upturned in a teasing grin.

"You think so, *ja?*"

Lilly's mouth sagged open, and she bit back a flood of hurt. *What an ego*. Lilly focused on the sharpening outline of the Clark farm.

Beside her, the German chuckled. She glared at him. He drove, eyes ahead, a loose smile playing on his lips. His powerful sunbaked forearms rested on the patched knees of his work pants as he fingered the reins, and he was so tall sitting beside her, she could hide inside his massive shadow. The absurdity of her protective act hit Lilly like a fist. This man was no prairie dog. No wonder he had laughed.

Lilly hung her head as a blush crept up her face.

Who was this man? Why was he here? Frustration blurted out her question. "What's your name?"

The German peeked at her and hesitated slightly before answering. "They call me Henry. Henry Zook.

"Henry Zook." Lilly twisted the name over her tongue.

"But my friends call me by my given name, Heinrick." He said it in a tone that made it sound like a request.

Lilly bit her lip. Friends? She wasn't, couldn't be his friend. A knot tightened in her stomach.

"Stop please!"

Heinrick yanked on the reins, and the horses skittered to a

stop. They were still a stone's throw from the Clark lane, but common sense screamed at her to leave, immediately.

"What is it?"

Lilly gathered her skirt and hauled herself over the side. Heinrick watched her without a word as she retrieved her basket. When Lilly glanced at him, however, his jaw hardened and he swallowed. Lilly stepped away and waited for him to drive off.

Heinrick made to slap the horses, then paused. He turned and looked at her, and a palpable sadness filled his eyes. Lilly felt a small place in her heart tear apart.

"Thank you," Heinrick said in a soft tone. Then he flicked the reins and trotted away.

five

"Mother, I'm back." Lilly swiped off her straw hat as the screen door slammed behind her.

Mother Clark entered the mudroom, wiping her hands on her patchwork apron. She scowled as she took the smashed basket from Lilly's hands.

"What happened to this?"

Lilly hung her hat on one of the pegs fastened to the wall. She steadied her voice, hoping it sounded close to normal. "I'm sorry, Mother. I dropped it."

Her mother first examined the basket, then she scrutinized Lilly's flushed face. Lilly offered a rueful smile and saw concern seep into her mother's brown eyes.

"Well," her mother said at last, "Go wash up. Dinner is almost prepared."

Lilly poured herself a bowl of water and washed off a sticky layer of prairie dust, as well as, she hoped, any indications of her outrageous behavior in town and the disturbing ride home. She freshly braided her hair and pronounced herself recovered, despite an odd soreness in her heart.

Dinner hour in the Clark home was as sacred as a church service. Lilly heard her father tramping about upstairs as he washed off the dirt from the fields and changed out of his grimy overalls. Her younger sister, Bonnie, hollered from the front door, and a moment later DJ and Frankie blew in from the yard like twisters. Lilly poured fresh milk into glasses while her mother removed a batch of biscuits from the wood-burning oven.

"Any news from town, Lilly?" Olive breezed in with a clean and chubby-faced Christian on her hip. Lilly's mouth went dry.

"Olive, could you please open a jar of pickles?" Mother Clark untied her headscarf and apron, hanging them on a hook near the mudroom door. Olive headed for the pantry, and Lilly licked her dry lips and felt her heartbeat restart. Maybe she could keep a lid on her latest reckless exploit.

Her father blew a feathery kiss across her mother's cheek, then took his position at the head of the table. The family gathered around him, leaving an opening where Olive's husband, Chuck, normally sat. Her mother set a bowl of gravy on the table and slid next to her husband on a long bench. Lilly noticed her father's face seemed drawn. After he asked the blessing, she discovered why.

"A drought is coming. I read it in the almanac, and I see it in the clear blue sky. No rain. The soil is drying up, and even the wheat I planted in last year's fallow field is withering."

Her mother slid a hand over her husband's clasped hands. Lilly noticed her father's green eyes seemed to age "We need to find a way to lay up stores for the winter. I don't think we'll make enough on the wheat to hold us through."

Her father couldn't tend the crop alone, and without Chuck's help, the eighty acres he'd added two years ago would revert to the bank.

Despite the beckoning aroma of beef sauced in onion and dill gravy, dinner went nearly untouched. Only Frankie and DJ dove into their food. Lilly wished, just this once, she had their naive trust.

Olive adjusted Christian on her knee and handed him a biscuit scrap. "I volunteered to help out at the armory, with Red Cross packages, but maybe I can find a job, instead. I know they're advertising for cooks at Fannie's boardinghouse."

Her father, who had been examining his fork, glanced at her and smiled. But his eyes spoke regret.

Lilly played with the fraying edge of her cotton napkin. "Mrs. Torgesen asked me to make her something for the Independence Day picnic," she said. "That will help." She peeked at her mother, who flashed a reassuring grin.

"We'll all work together and put it into the Lord's hands," her father quietly summed up. The matter was dropped, but apprehension lingered as the shadows stretched out in dusty patterns along the kitchen floor.

&

"Have you lost your senses, or are you *trying* to destroy your life?" Olive added a hiss to her furious whisper.

Lilly clasped her hands and sat still as stone on the straight-back chair. News traveled like a lightning bolt across the prairie and, as Olive marched out her fury on the clapboard floor of Lilly's second-story bedroom, Lilly knew her rash behavior in town had ignited.

Olive bounced little Christian over to her other hip. Christian giggled at the bumpy ride. The two year old loosened a strand of his mother's chestnut brown hair, unraveling the bun at the nape of her neck, to match Olive's demeanor. Her sister had stomped home an hour earlier, her after-dinner stroll with Elizabeth White destroyed by "a sordid tale that involved Lilly cavorting with a stranger in town."

"You have no idea who that man is, nor where he is from. He could have hurt you!" Olive's voice rose a pitch. Lilly winced. "You stepped into a fight that was none of your business! I heard the Craffeys caught him stealing—he had two apples in his coat pocket!"

"He wasn't wearing a coat, Olive."

"And he spoke a different language—like he was demon-possessed!"

Olive paused in her tirade to plunk Christian down on the double bed Lilly shared with Bonnie. Christian rolled across the quilt, drooling.

Lilly sucked a calming breath of air. "Olive, listen. I admit my foolishness." She held up her hands in surrender. "I won't do it again."

Olive bent down and glared into Lilly's face. "You bet you won't. Because if you do, I'll tell Chuck. . .and he'll tell Reggie!"

Lilly recoiled as if she'd been slapped. Her sister's threat hung in the air like an odor. Lilly willed her voice steady. "Don't worry, Olive. I don't even know who he is. I'll never talk to him again, I promise."

Olive clamped her hands onto her narrow hips. "You better not, or you'll be sorry." She scooped up Christian. "Reggie doesn't need distractions, Lilly. Do you want to get him killed?"

Lilly gasped. Olive stormed out, slamming the bedroom door behind her.

Lilly closed her eyes. "Please God, no." She hadn't considered that perhaps God would punish her for helping the German. Perhaps He, too, considered her a traitor. But would He let Reggie die because she'd sinned?

Lilly fought the insidious idea and walked over to the window seat. The cushion in the alcove was one of her first sewing projects, a calico pillow in blue and yellow. Lilly climbed into the nook, pulled her knees to her chest, and rested her head on her crossed arms. The prairie stretched to the far horizon, forever past the hundred and twenty acres that belonged to the Clark family. The sun painted the wheat field hues of rose gold and the hay field to the north a jade green. Her father would begin haying soon, cutting the grass, letting it dry, and gathering it up into giant mounds for cattle feed during the winter.

Was it only two years ago she'd worked with Reggie, mowing the hay? She smiled at the image of his serious brown eyes, the sun baking his back and arms. Even then, he'd wanted to protect her. "Lilly-girl, you shouldn't be working here. This is men's work." She wanted to cry. After all he'd done for her, and she'd betrayed him.

Oh God, please send him home! If Reggie were here, perhaps he'd be working with Chuck, dragging in water from the Missouri to keep the crop alive.

The front door slammed, and she watched her father stride out to the barn, heading for the evening milking. The Clarks had two dozen Holstein her father used to run a fairly lucrative dairy route on the west side of the Missouri to the ranchers who didn't raise milkers.

But if the prairie dried up, so would their Holsteins. Lilly's eyes burned. The threat of drought made her escapade in town seem all the worse.

"I'm sorry, Reggie, I'm sorry." Had she really betrayed him? Lilly pressed her fists into her eyes, but she couldn't erase the clear image of Heinrick, hands up in surrender, backing away from the Craffey boys, jabbering incoherently. Nor could she forget the tone of longing in his voice when he'd offered his name in friendship. No, she hadn't done anything wrong; she'd merely performed a Christian duty of kindness. At least she hoped that was true. She hoped she hadn't somehow stepped over the line of faithfulness to Reggie or to her country and summoned punishment from the Almighty for her misbehavior. Dread seeped into her bones.

"Please forgive me, God," she moaned feebly.

She would never see the German again. Lilly resolved it in her heart, to herself, to Reggie, and finally to God.

six

"Please, Mrs. Torgesen, just two more pins." Lilly snatched a straight pin from the corner of her mouth while she struggled with the flimsy newspaper pattern.

Mrs. Torgesen, wiggling about as if she were a two year old, held the latest edition of the *Ladies Home Journal* and flipped from page to page as if window-shopping in Boston.

"Oh, this eggshell blue chiffon is just breathtaking! How long did you say it would take to order?"

Lilly stifled a groan as another page tore across Mrs. Torgesen's ample backside. Doggedly, she pinned it together. "Two weeks, earliest."

Mrs. Torgesen sighed, then glanced down at Lilly. "Well, how's it coming?"

Lilly managed a smile. "Do you want pleats or gathers?"

Mrs. Torgesen hopped off the tiny stool, and Lilly heard the remainder of her pattern rip to shreds. She sighed and conceded defeat. Mrs. Torgesen would change it three or four times before completion, anyway. Lilly stuck the pins into her wrist cushion and collected the scraps of paper.

"How about this one?" Mrs. Torgesen held out the magazine, pointing to a picture of a two-tiered gown in muted lavender. The skirt slid to just below the knees, with wide pleated rows running hip to hip. An underskirt, in the same shade, continued to the ankles. The bodice was a simple white cotton blouse with puffed sleeves and a boat-style neck. What made the piece stunning was the sheer lace lavender overcoat that covered the blouse and flared out over the hips. The ensemble was then secured with a wide satin belt, accentuated on the side with a six-inch satin rosebud.

"How exquisite." Lilly passed back the magazine.

"Make it for me, Lilly. I know you can." Mrs. Torgesen rained a toothy grin down on her. Lilly smiled as if she couldn't wait, but she wanted to grimace. The woman would be a giant purple poppy. .

Lilly stood up. "Let's see what you have for fabric. Maybe I can do it from scraps."

"You know where the fabric is, Dear." Mrs. Torgesen patted her glistening brow with a lace-edged handkerchief. "I need a glass of lemonade." She waddled off toward the kitchen.

Lilly always thought Mrs. Torgesen could be described by one word: excessive. She was a woman who couldn't be contained—or contain anything, including her appetite for food and clothing. She lived with one foot dangling in the waters of lavishness and laughed away the criticism of brow-raising conservatives from the North Dakota border on down. Yet all tolerated Mrs. Torgesen, despite her fanciful ideas, and Lilly supposed it was for one very large reason—the breadth and strength of the Torgesen T cattle ranch.

Lilly slipped off her wrist cushion and tucked it inside her sewing box. She considered it a blessing to be employed by Mrs. Torgesen—not only did it allow her to work with feather-fine silk, transparent chambray, and filmy chiffon, but Mrs. Torgesen's dreams pushed Lilly's skills to new heights. And, despite Mrs. Torgesen's desire to dress like a French dame, her generosity had helped Lilly finance her wedding dress and prepare for the event she knew her father would struggle to provide. And now, the work could help keep the Clark family fed.

Lilly headed upstairs to the sewing room. Mrs. Torgesen couldn't even sew a straight stitch, but she owned a gleaming black Singer. Lilly preferred, however, to bring her work home and sew in the comfort of her bedroom, laying the pattern out on the hardwood floor or on the kitchen table. And, at home, her mother was always available for advice.

The high sun spilled through the yellow calico curtains, lighting the corner room in an array of cheery colors.

The remnant fabric was stuffed into a three-door oak

wardrobe. The doors creaked as they opened, the wood split from years of dry prairie heat. Lilly wrinkled her nose against the pungent odor of mothballs and dove in, wading through a sea of jeweled fabrics from dyed wool in jade and mauve to calicos in every shade of blue.

Lilly finally unearthed five yards of plain, sea foam green cotton and a piece of white flowered lace large enough for the overcoat. Perhaps she could dye it. Tucked in the back, behind a piece of red calico, she pulled out a forest green satin, perhaps meant for a pillow edge. It would make a perfect sash. Mrs. Torgesen would be a flowing willow, drifting along Main Street on Independence Day. Lilly stifled a chuckle.

Lilly was piling the fabric pieces onto a small box table next to the Singer when movement in the yard below caught her eye.

The sight of a golden mustang, bucking and writhing beneath its rider in the sunbaked corral made her step toward the window. The animal's black eyes bulged with terror as the cowboy atop the bronc whooped, grabbed the saddle horn, and spurred the horse. The mustang reared, then threw himself forward and bucked, flaying out his hind legs. Sweat flicked off his body. Lilly stood transfixed at the desperate wrestle.

Suddenly, the cowboy dropped one of the split reins. Lilly winced as she watched him grab for the saddle horn. His whooping had stopped and only her thundering heart filled the silence as the horse bucked and kicked, twisting under its mount. Then, with a violent snap, the mustang pitched the cowboy into the air. Lilly watched him climb the sky in an airborne sprawl. He flew a good ten feet and landed with a poof of prairie smoke.

The mustang continued to twist, jump, and kick in a hysterical dance. His wide hooves landed closer to the hapless cowboy with each furious snort. All at once, the animal reared, pawing the air above the terrified rider. The man wrapped his arms around his head, curled into a ball, and waited to be trampled.

Lilly covered her eyes and peeked through her fingers.

Suddenly, a figure erupted from the barn door. A blond whirlwind, he burst right up to the furious animal. Holding out both hands as if to embrace the beast, he closed quickly and in a lightning motion snared the dangling reins and planted his feet. The downed cowboy scrambled toward the barn.

The mustang reared and snorted. The man extended his hand to catch the horse's line of vision. The horse jerked his head and pawed at the ground, but with each snort, the terror dissipated, his feet calming their erratic dance until, in one long exhale, he stopped prancing altogether. The man brought a steady hand close to the horse's eye. The mustang bobbed his head twice, then let his captor touch his velvet nose. After a moment, the man stepped close and rubbed the bronc between his eyes and over his jaw.

Lilly exhaled and realized she'd been holding her breath. Whoever he was, the cowboy had a way with animals that tugged at her heart and stole her breath. As she watched, the man turned and looked toward the house. The sun glinted in his blue eyes, and he wore an unmistakable half-smile. Lilly jumped away from the window. Her heart did an erratic tumble in her chest, and her skin turned to goose-flesh. Despite her vow, she'd somehow found Heinrick.

≈

Lilly heaped the fabric into a ball, scooped it into her arms, and scrambled downstairs. Her heart flopped like a freshly netted fish, dazed and horrified at the recent turn of events. The last thing she needed was a reminder of yesterday's scandalous incident. She would keep her head down and flee like a jackrabbit from the Torgesen T and its troublesome German.

"Ma, I don't think Buttercup is the right name for that mustang!" Clive Torgesen slammed the screen door and dragged a trail of prairie dust into the kitchen. Lilly skidded to a halt in the doorway, clutching the fabric to her chest. She didn't realize it had been Clive, Mrs. Torgesen's uncouth son, who had ridden the terrorized animal. At best, Clive was a roadblock to a speedy, unsuspicious escape; at worst, he would smear her with one of his crude remarks and recount yesterday's embarrassing tale in embellished detail. Lilly gritted her teeth and sidled out of view.

The fair-haired Torgesen boy was one of the lucky—he'd been granted a bye in the enlistment lottery. Some thought it was because he was Ed Torgesen's only son. Others believed it had something to do with a wad of George Washingtons in the county registrar's back pocket. Nevertheless, Clive Torgesen was now one of the few, and of them the most, eligible bachelors in the state.

To Lilly's way of thinking, that wasn't saying much. Underneath the ruggedly handsome exterior—his curly, sandy-blond hair, his earth brown eyes, and his heavy-duty muscles—was a completely rotten core. As her father liked to say, "There was a foul smell to that bird's stuffin'." Lilly had the unfortunate experience of sitting next to Clive in school. She'd seen his pranks firsthand, from cutting off the braids of little girls to throwing youngsters into the Missouri River in October. Now older, he was downright dangerous. Lilly had heard the gossip, seen the faces of girls he'd "courted," and doubted the honor of the man in the wide-brimmed black Stetson.

Clive plopped down in a willow-backed chair next to his mother at the kitchen table. The housekeeper, Eleanor, served him a sweating glass of lemonade, and he guzzled it down.

Mrs. Torgesen dabbed at her forehead with her handkerchief. "Your father thinks the mustang will make a wonderful stallion. He is expecting two brood mares from Wyoming in a week or so."

"Well, he's impossible to ride. He ought to be hobbled."

"Hobbled!" Lilly cried and burst through the door. "What he needs is a gentle hand, Clive."

Clive sat back in his chair and tipped up his hat with one long, grimy finger. "Well, Lilly Clark. Since when are you the expert on wild horses?"

Lilly clamped her mouth shut. Her face burned, and she

wanted to melt through the polished clapboard floor. Mrs. Torgesen leveled a curious frown at her. Lilly swallowed, and held out the fabric to Mrs. Torgesen. "I think I found something that might work," she croaked.

Mrs. Torgesen turned her attention back to Clive. "Give him a week or so, Dear. He'll settle down. Pick a different horse."

Clive snuffed. "I almost had him broke, too, Ma. Until that stupid German interfered."

Mrs. Torgesen peeked at Eleanor, then drilled a sharp look into Clive. "He's not German, Clive. He's from Norway, just like us."

Clive's eyes narrowed, squeezing out something unpleasant. An eerie silence embedded the room while Clive and Mrs. Torgesen sipped their lemonade and glowered at each other. Lilly glanced at Eleanor, but she busily stirred a pot of bubbling jam on the stove. The sharp, sweet smell of strawberries saturated the humid air.

Clive gulped the last of his drink. He examined the glass, turning it in his hand. "Well, whatever he is, he's a troublemaker, and I'd keep my eye on him if I was you, Ma."

Mrs. Torgesen slid a dimpled hand onto Clive's arm. "That's why you're the foreman."

Clive emitted a loud "humph." He set the glass on the table and ran a finger around the edge. "So that means I can do what I want with him, right?"

"It's your crew, Dear."

Clive smiled, but evil prowled about his dark eyes. He stood and tipped his hat to Lilly. "See ya 'round." He winked at her as he turned away.

The bile rose in the back of Lilly's throat.

Mrs. Torgesen sighed. "Let me see the fabric, Lilly."

The next two hours crawled by as Lilly fashioned a makeshift pattern from a remnant piece of muslin. The costume would require a mile of fabric, it seemed, and Mrs. Torgesen would bake in it under the hot summer sun, but she obviously had no regard for such discomforts.

"I want it ready by the Fourth of July."

Lilly pushed a rebel strand of brown hair behind her ear. One week. "Yes, Ma'am."

ॐ

The low sun tinged the clouds with gold and amber as Lilly plodded home. Three miles to go and her arms screamed from the weight of the small mountain of fabric. But the wind was fresh on her face and not only had she avoided another perilous run-in with the German, but neither Mrs. Torgesen nor Clive hinted Lilly might know him. Either they hadn't heard or they were hoping she'd keep their secrets if they kept hers.

A hawk circled above, and Lilly heard Reggie's voice, strong and wise, in her head. *Watch the hawk, Lilly, it will lead you to dinner.* She didn't do much hunting, but somehow his words stuck in her memory. Just like his firm hand upon the small of her back, or nimble fingers playing with her hair. She could never forget his kiss—just one, on an eve such as this, as the sun slid behind the bluffs beyond the river. She and Reggie had strolled to her favorite refuge, a tiny retreat nestled in a grove of maples. There, he told her he would marry her. He didn't have anything to give her, he said, "but his promise." Then he cupped her face in his strong hands and kissed her.

He'd left for the war the next day, yet she could still feel his thumb caressing her cheek, feel his lips upon hers. *Oh Reggie, please come home soon.*

The creak of a buckboard scattered her memories. At a hot breath over her shoulder, Lilly gasped and sprang into the weeds lining the dirt road. Laughter, rich, deep, and unpretentious, filled the air. Lilly whirled, squinting into the sunlight.

"Hello. We meet again." Heinrick greeted her with a sweeping white smile and twinkling blue eyes.

Lilly's heart raced like a jackrabbit eluding prey.

"Want a ride?"

Lilly shook her head.

"C'mon. I can repay you for saving me." His grin seemed mischievous.

"I thought you said you didn't need saving." Lilly shut her impulsive mouth and squeezed the fabric to her chest.

He raised his eyebrows. "Did I say that?"

Lilly frowned. Had he? It didn't matter. She wasn't getting into a buckboard with an enemy of the community. She'd vowed it to Reggie and to God, and she wasn't going to break her promise.

"I don't want a ride." Lilly stepped into the road and started walking, her legs moving in crisp, quick rhythm. "Thank you, anyway."

Heinrick followed her, the horses meandering down the road.

"Go away, Mr. Zook!" Lilly called over her shoulder, annoyance pricking her.

"My friends call me Heinrick!"

"I'm not your friend."

He did not immediately reply, and Lilly felt the sting of her words. The locusts hissed from the surrounding fields, their disapproval snared and carried to her by an unrelenting prairie wind. Lilly pounded out her steps in silence, her knuckles white as she clutched the fabric.

"Why not?"

Lilly stopped and whirled on her heels. "Because you are German! And if you haven't noticed, America is in a war against Germany! My fiancé, Reggie, is over there," she flung her arm out eastward, "trying not to get killed by your countrymen. I can hardly accept a ride from a man who may have relatives shooting my future husband at this very moment!" She sucked a breath of dry, searing air and willed her heart to calm. "That, Mr. Zook, is why I can't be your friend."

She saw a glimmer of hope die in his eyes with her painful words, and Heinrick's misshapen grin slowly vanished. A shard of regret sliced through her. She wasn't a rude person, but she had no choice but to be brutally frank.

They were at war, America and Germany, she and Heinrick. And war was ruthless.

"Please, just leave me alone," Lilly pleaded.

Heinrick nodded slowly. "I understand." His eyes hardened. "But that's going to be a bit hard, seeing we both work for the Torgesens."

"Try, please, or you're going to get us both into a mess of trouble."

He leveled an even, piercing gaze on her. "I am sorry, *Fraulein*. Trouble is the last thing I hope to bring you. I'd much prefer to bring you flowers." Then he slapped the horses and took off in a fast trot.

Lilly gaped as she watched him ride away, his muscular back strong and proud against a withering prairie backdrop. Then her throat began to burn, and by the time she neared her house, she was wiping away a sheet of tears.

seven

An early afternoon sun cast ringlets of light through Lilly's eyelet curtains and across her vanity. Her brown hair was swept up into a neat braided bun, and a slight breeze, tinged with the smell of fresh lily of the valley, played with the tendrils of hair curling around her ears. Lilly bent over her parchment, scribing her words.

June 28, 1918

My Dearest Reggie,

My thoughts were with you this morning as we walked to church. DJ, who'd lingered behind us, startled a ring-necked pheasant into flight, and I recalled the year when you found an entire nest and gave us three for Thanksgiving dinner. I also remember Harley's envy that year when you brought in two bucks to his doe. I am counting on your aim to protect you and Chuck and can't help but shiver with you when I think of you huddling in the foxholes. I haven't said a word to Olive, who, I fear, believes you all within the safety of a fortified Paris. Perhaps it's for the best; she and little Chris prefer the cheerful reports from the censored Milwaukee Journal.

On to glad news. The city fathers have agreed to preserve tradition and host the Mobridge rodeo on Independence Day. In the absence of many regular participants, they have extended an invitation to the children, allowing them to compete in the center ring. Frankie is hilarious with joy. He commandeered Father's plow and spent the last week practicing his steer roping. As Father won't let him near the cows, Sherlock became his unfortunate victim. Frank stood upon the plow, flung about him the lasso you constructed, and then wrestled

the hapless spaniel to the dirt. After three days of tireless prac-
tice, Sherlock finally crawled behind the lattice under the back
porch, and since Friday has refused to reappear. Twice I saw
Mother slide a bowl of scraps under the steps; I believe she has
more than an ounce of empathy for the old pup!

The prairie is already beginning to wilt; the black-eyed
Susans and goldenrod, which were so vibrant only a month
ago, have joined the fraying weeds. The heat this year is
insufferable, and I know if you were here, I'd find you in the
Missouri, fighting the catfish for space. Do you miss the river
and the song of the crickets at dusk? I can't imagine what
France must be like—does it have coyotes or prairie dogs or
cottonwoods to remind you of home?

Marjorie is distraught over Harley's cold. I hope he is
recovering and has rejoined you in the trenches, not that I
wish any of you there; rather I would have you all here. But
I know how you must miss him, and I can't bear to imagine
you alone during an offensive. May God watch over you.

Mother and Father send their love. I talked to your father
in town two weeks ago, and he looked fit and calm, as is his
nature. His courageous, faithful prayers continually inspire
me; my own petitions seem so feeble in comparison. Nevertheless, my thoughts are constantly upon you and the pledge
we made in the shadow of the maples near the bluff. Please
come home to me.

> Faithfully,
> Lillian

Lilly folded the page, slid it into a creamy white envelope,
and propped it against her round mirror. She hadn't mentioned Heinrick, and a sliver of deceit pierced her heart. But,
why should she? She'd hardly mentioned the drought, either,
for Reggie's own good. She didn't want him to worry, and
neither did she want him to imagine a scenario that had never
existed, would never exist, between her and Heinrick. Better
to let the matter die in the dust. If he ever did ask, she would

tell him she'd merely saved a man from a good pummeling.

She heard the screen door slam, then voices drift toward her room. Her heart skipped. The Larsens, and perhaps they had news from Reggie!

Or, and her smile fell at the thought, maybe they had news about her. So far, no one other than Olive had hinted a word about the event in Mobridge, already almost a week past. But, then again, her parents were busy people and didn't cotton to gossip. Unless, of course, it involved their daughter.

Lilly gulped a last bit of peaceful air, painted a smile on her face, and bounced down the stairs.

Rev. and Mrs. Larsen sat in two padded green Queen Anne chairs in the parlor, glasses of lemonade sweating in their hands. Rev. Larsen rose and greeted her. Lilly smoothed her white cotton dress, glad she hadn't changed after church, and sat next to her mother on a faded blue divan.

"So, news from Reggie?" she asked and tried to ignore the tremor in her voice.

Mrs. Alice Larsen shook her head. "Simply a social call to our future daughter-in-law and her parents."

Lilly grinned. The coast was clear, no storms brewing on the horizon. Olive sauntered into the room, little Chris on her hip, still in his Buster Brown church uniform. She waggled his pudgy arm at the small crowd. "Going for a nap," she said in a baby voice, then backed out of the room. She glanced at Lilly, who caught the scorching look, as if in reprimand, from her older sister.

"Reggie wrote and told us that you're planning to join the Red Cross?" Rev. Larsen asked Lilly.

Lilly shrugged. "Oh, that was just talk. I'm not sure right now."

"Well, I heard they need volunteers. It sounds like the work is endless." It seemed Rev. Larsen knew everyone's needs, business, and talents. At least those of his congregation. "I am sure Reggie would be proud."

Lilly blushed.

"Lilly's been doing a lot of sewing, especially for the Torgesen family." Her mother winked at Lilly.

Mrs. Larsen dabbed a lace-trimmed kerchief on her neck. "It's so nice that you can help out your family, and sewing is such a needed talent in the church. It will serve you well as a pastor's wife."

"Lilly has much to offer to help Reggie get a firm hold on a nice flourishing congregation when he returns."

Lilly shot a glance at her father. She suddenly felt like a prize milking cow, up on the auction block.

"That is, until she starts filling the house with babies." Mrs. Larsen cocked her head and slathered Lilly with soupy eyes. "I can't wait to be a grandmother."

"So Reggie is going into the ministry after the war?" Lilly's mother rose to refill the half-empty glasses.

Rev. Larsen nodded. "He's all ready to follow in his father's footsteps." He held out his glass. "But I won't be handing over the pulpit too quickly. He'll have to tuck some experience under his belt first. Maybe take on a smaller church, perhaps up north in Eureka, or plant a missionary church over in Java, that new Russian community."

Lilly stared past them at the patterned floral wallpaper her mother had lugged west from her home in Illinois. Her mother had been a banker's daughter, brought up on fine linens and satin draperies. Life on the prairie had toughened her hands and character, but her refined, padded childhood still lingered in her choice of home decor. Lace curtains blew at the open window, and a portrait of Lilly's stately maternal grandparents hung on the wall over the rolltop desk. Lilly often wondered who her mother had been before she'd met Donald Clark, before he'd moved her to the prairie, and before life with blizzards, drought, and birthing five children etched crow's-feet into her creamy face.

"Lilly, are you listening?" Her mother's voice pierced her musings.

"What?"

"Mrs. Larsen asked you if you'd started your wedding dress yet."

Mrs. Larsen leaned forward in her chair. A thick silence swelled through the room. The tick of the clock chipped out eternal seconds.

"Uh, well, no, actually. I felt I should wait."

With her words, the fear about Reggie's future ignited. The questions, the fears, the unknowns. With one bullet, one misstep in the no-man's-land between battle lines, their hopes would die. Mrs. Larsen gasped, her eyes filled, and she held a shaking hand to her lips.

Lilly hung her head. "I'm sorry."

Maybe she should start on her wedding dress, as much for her own sake as Mrs. Larsen's. Maybe that was just what she needed to get her focus back on the plan and erase the memory of her traitorous encounter with Heinrick. The fact that she easily conjured up his crooked smile or those dancing blue eyes bothered her more than she wanted to admit.

"Thank you for the lovely sermon today, Reverend." Mrs. Clark filled the silence. Rev. Larsen leaned back into the molded chair. It creaked. "Thank you, Ruth. The passage about Abraham and Isaac is such a difficult one to interpret."

Her father threw in his chip as if to reassure the preacher. "You did well, helping us to remember it was Abraham's obedience that won Isaac back to him. He obeyed God, regardless of the cost; that's what is important."

Rev. Larsen nodded. "That's what I continue to tell our young people," and he fastened steel eyes on Lilly, adopting his preaching tone, "Obedience to God and to the church is the only sure path in this world. If they want to find peace, they will walk it without faltering."

Lilly smiled meekly and noticed he'd balled his free hand on his lap, most likely a reflex action. Unfortunately, the Clark parlor had no pulpit to pound.

"Take Ruth, for example," he continued, his voice adopting

a singing quality. "She, without a husband, obeyed her vows, despite the fact that it would mean a life without children, and followed Naomi to a foreign land. And God gave her Boaz and blessed her for her obedience."

" 'Obedience is better than sacrifice,' Samuel told Saul," added Mrs. Larsen.

"That's right, Dear." The reverend tightened his lips and nodded.

Bonnie entered the room with a plate of shortbread. Her mother took it from her and served the guests. "But what about faith? Wasn't it because of Abraham's faith that God counted him righteous?"

Lilly shot a quizzical look at her mother.

"Of course!" Rev. Larsen stabbed his finger in the air as if her mother had made his point. "Obedience is faith. It's faith in action. If we want to show God that we love Him, we will obey. And then, He will bless us—reward us for our faithfulness. Our obedience assures us of God's blessings and of His love."

Rev. Larsen shifted his gaze to Lilly's father. "That is why so many of our youth have problems today. They abandon the teachings of their church and parents. Without guidance, their lives simply run amuck."

Her father nodded soberly.

"But not your Lilly, here." Every eye turned toward Lilly. "I always told Reggie that Lilly would make a fine wife. I've watched her since her childhood, especially while Reggie was at school, and decided she would have no problem being a submissive, obedient wife. I told Reggie so when he returned from college." He leaned forward, balancing his elbows on both knees, and pinned her with a sincere look. "I'm glad he listened to me."

Lilly forced a smile. Had Reggie chosen her because of his father? No, Reggie said he'd been chasing her since her bloomer days. She couldn't believe the look in Reggie's eyes was anything but true love. Besides, she *would* be a good wife. She would see to that herself. She had no intention of falling off the path of the straight and narrow and landing "amuck," as Rev. Larsen so delicately stated it. She knew her path in life, and when God brought Reggie home, she would start walking down it.

Lilly saw Mrs. Larsen dab at her forehead. She suddenly became conscious of her own glistening brow and the oppressive heat that filtered through the lace from the prairie. It oozed into her pores, flowed under her skin, and bubbled in a place inside her body. The pictures of her grandparents spun at odd angles.

"Will you excuse me, please?" Lilly rose to her feet, reaching out her hand to grasp the back of her chair.

"Lilly, are you ill?" Her mother put down the tray.

Lilly shook her head. "I just feel a bit hot and dizzy."

"By all means, go lie down." Mrs. Larsen had also risen, concern on her pale face. Somehow, the woman managed to avoid the sun despite living in a virtual oven.

"Thank you for coming, Rev. Larsen, Mrs. Larsen." Lilly fingered her temple, as if her head were throbbing. But as she exited the parlor and felt a cool breeze filter in from the kitchen, she realized it wasn't dizziness that had attacked her in the parlor. . .it felt more like the numbing grasp of suffocation.

eight

The week before Independence Day passed in a flurry of fabric, needles, and fittings. Lilly hiked out to the Torgesen ranch three times during the week to fit the skirt, then the bodice, and finally the end product.

She couldn't help but look for Heinrick. His presence at the Torgesen T was a magnet, and despite the warnings in her heart, Lilly couldn't stop herself from scanning the horizon as she left the ranch, certain she would see him and strangely disappointed when she didn't. Of course, if she had, she would have ignored him, but still, the fact that he seemed to be avoiding her registered an odd despondency in her heart.

Mrs. Torgesen did resemble a willow tree. Lilly's mother dug up a half-bottle of Christmas dye, and Lilly colored the lace overcoat a rose leaf green. The three shades of green blended into a pleasing harmony, and Mrs. Torgesen bubbled with delight as she sashayed around the kitchen during the final fitting.

"Lilly, Dear, fetch the millinery box from the parlor, will you? I want you to see the new hat I ordered from Chicago. It came on yesterday's train."

Yesterday's train! Lilly had been so busy, she'd forgotten about the mail train the day before. Her heart pounded as she retrieved the hatbox. There might be a letter from Reggie waiting in her mailbox right now.

Lilly set the box down on the kitchen table. Mrs. Torgesen opened it and wiggled out a wide-brimmed, purposely misshapen hat. It was long and oval, meant to be propped low and sideways on Mrs. Torgesen's head. The brim curled like an upturned lip in the back and sported three layers of transparent white lace wound around the bowl. A flurry of leftover

51

lace dangled from the back like a tail. The crowning feature of Mrs. Torgesen's new hat was a molded bluebird, nestled in the lacey layers and snuggled up to the shallow bowl of the hat in the front. Lilly swallowed a laugh—a bird in the willow! Mrs. Torgesen plopped the hat on her blond head and tied the mauve satin sash under her chin.

"Well?"

Lilly shook her head slowly. "Amazing."

Mrs. Torgesen glowed. "Well, just because one lives in the middle of a wasteland doesn't mean one has to blend!" She let out a hearty laugh, as did Lilly. The one thing Erica Torgesen *didn't* do was "blend."

≈

The sun was still a high brilliant orb as Lilly stepped out into the Torgesen yard. Mrs. Torgesen had paid her well, and Lilly headed for town to pick up more sugar for her mother's currant jam, also planning a quick stop at the post office.

Lilly tugged on the brim of her straw hat and tucked her basket into the crook of her arm. A hot breeze whipped past her and brought with it a horse's whinny. Lilly shot a glance toward the corral just in time to sight a cowboy riding in astride a magnificent bay. The man didn't notice her. His shoulders sagged as if from exhaustion, and dust layered him like a second skin. But, as he dismounted, Lilly plainly recognized Heinrick. She gasped and reined in her traitorous heart. Her feet seemed rooted to the ground. Heinrick looped the horse's reins over the fence and turned toward the house.

In a breathless moment, Heinrick's eyes fastened upon her, and a wave of shock washed over his face. It seemed as though, in that instant, some film fell away from him and she could see him clearly, unfettered by prejudice and stereotypes. He was a man etching out a life on the prairie, building simple hopes, maybe a home and a family, just like every pioneer before him. The sense of it overwhelmed her, shredding her resolve to turn a hard eye to him. Trembling, Lilly bit her lower lip and blinked back tears.

A smile nipped at the corners of Heinrick's mouth. She waited for it to materialize into fullness, but he abruptly extinguished it and offered a curt nod instead, tugging on the brim of his hat. He didn't move, however. They stood there, fifteen feet apart, staring at each other, and Lilly felt the gulf of an entire ocean between them. The desire to tell him she was sorry and ask how he was doing pulsed inside her. But she stayed mute.

Heinrick finally pulled off his leather gloves, tucked them into his chaps, and turned away from her. She watched him lumber toward the bunkhouse, feeling in his wake the weight of his loneliness.

She carried it all the way into Mobridge.

❧

Independence Day preparations had sparked the town into activity. Westward, near the Missouri, Lilly spied the makings of the Fourth of July fair: unfamiliar rigs, buckboards, tents, and various prize livestock. On the other end of town, stood makeshift cattle pens and a large corral. In two days, cowboys from all over South Dakota would gather to duke it out with untamed beasts in the Mobridge rodeo. Lilly loved the exotic, recaptured display of bygone days from a now-tamed West. Reggie always participated as a hazer for his authentic cowboy buddies. A rugged memory hit her like a warm gust of wind. In his nut-brown leather cowboy hat, the one with the Indian braid dangling down the back, and his fringed sandy-colored chaps, Reggie easily passed for a ranch hand, and a dashing one, besides.

Despite the fresh ache of Reggie's absence, Lilly knew Mobridge desperately needed the rodeo and the mind-numbing gaiety of Independence Day. They needed to celebrate with gusto, to remind themselves why they sacrificed, all of them—mothers, sons, wives, and husbands. They were at war to make the world safe for freedom, for independence.

Lilly jumped at the *hee-haw* of a late model Packard. She skittered to the side of the street and watched a mustard yellow Roadster roll by, the *oohs* and *aahs* of admiring farmers rolling out like a red carpet before it. Lilly smirked. Clive's Model T wouldn't be the only attraction in town over the holiday.

Ernestine's burst with shoppers, most of whom had unfamiliar tanned faces. A handful of Russian women, their wide, red faces glistening under colorfully dyed headscarves, haggled with Willard over a batch of home-canned sauerkraut and pickles. Their jumbled words stirred a memory within Lilly, and at once, Heinrick's sharp, strange mother tongue filled her mind. She fought the image of his tired eyes and sagging shoulders.

"What do you want today, Lilly?" Ernestine barked.

"Two pounds of sugar, please?"

Ernestine pinched her lips and searched under the wooden countertop for an extra burlap bag. She filled it with sugar and passed it over to Lilly. "Bring the bag back."

Lilly paid Ernestine, turned, and plowed straight into Marjorie's mother, Jennifer Pratt.

"Be careful, Girl!" Mrs. Pratt exclaimed.

Lilly blushed. "Excuse me, Mrs. Pratt."

Mrs. Pratt's voice softened. "How are you, Lilly?"

"Fine, thank you. How is Marjorie?"

"She's at the armory. Why don't you stop in and ask her yourself?"

Lilly tried not to notice the stares of three other women who had turned curious eyes upon her as soon as Mrs. Pratt announced her name. Shame swept through her bones.

"I'll do that," she mumbled. "Good day, Ma'am."

Mrs. Pratt nodded and moved past her. Lilly made for the door.

She stopped next at the post office. Lilly's heart did a small skip when the clerk handed her not only a letter from Reggie, but also one for Olive, from Chuck. Her sister would be ecstatic. She tucked both into the pocket of her apron as she crossed the street and headed to the armory.

The former one-room tavern swam with the odor of mothballs, cotton fibers, and antiseptic. A handful of uniformed girls ripped long strips of cloth.

Marjorie appeared every inch a Red Cross volunteer as she cut and wound long sheets of muslin and assembled first aid kits to send to the front. Over her calico prairie dress, she wore a standard-issue Red Cross white cotton pinafore, with two enormous pockets sewn into the skirt. Pinned on her head was a fabric-covered pillbox hat emblazoned with a bright red cross on the upturned crown.

"Lilly!" Marjorie dropped her fabric onto a long table and embraced her friend. "Did you hear the news?"

"What news?"

Marjorie's eyes twinkled. "Harley proposed."

"What?"

Marjorie grinned. "His last letter said he couldn't keep fighting without knowing I was pledged to him and our future. We'll be married as soon as he returns."

"But Marj, what if he doesn't come back?" Lilly instantly clamped a hand over her mouth, wishing her words back.

Marjorie gaped at her. "How can you say that? Of course he'll be back."

"I'm so sorry. Please forgive me."

Marjorie's anger dissolved, and she gathered Lilly into a forgiving hug. "No harm done. I know you're worried, too."

Tears pooled like a flash flood, spilling from Lilly's eyes. "I keep telling myself Reggie will be all right," she whispered. "I just wish I knew for sure that he would come home."

Marjorie looped her arm through Lilly's. She led her away from curious ears. "Let's not think about it. There is nothing we can do anyway. We just have to wait."

Lilly wiped the tears with her fingertips, already feeling her composure returning. But they had left their mark. Obviously, she missed Reggie more than she realized. She hadn't cried over him since receiving his last letter.

The pair stared out of a grimy window onto the street, at women lugging loaded baskets and dirt-streaked children running with hoops. Morrie stood in his doorway, his apron stained with shaving cream and strands of hair. A pack of cowboys emerged from Flanner's café. Some straddled their horses while another group surrounded the Packard, wishing for a more sophisticated form of transportation.

"By the way, are you all right?"

"What?" Lilly glanced at Marjorie and frowned.

"You can tell me, Lilly. Did he force you to help him?"

Lilly peeled her arm from Marjorie's grasp. "What are you talking about?"

Marjorie's eyes darted away, then back to Lilly. She lowered her voice. "The foreigner. I heard all about it from my sister. She said he grabbed you and forced you to drive him home."

So that was the local story. Or, at least one version of it. She shook her head. "That's not how it happened, Marj."

Marjorie paled. "What do you mean, Lilly? Did something else happen?"

Lilly held her friend's hands. "Listen, I will only say this once because, frankly, I am trying to forget it happened. The Craffey boys attacked Heinrick. It was unprovoked, no matter what anyone says, and entirely mismatched. I felt sorry for him, so I butted in."

Marjorie's eyes widened. "Heinrick?"

Lilly's face heated. "Forget I told you. I've already forgotten it and him."

Marjorie peered at her friend, as if seeing into her soul. "You don't look like you've forgotten it, Lilly. You're blushing."

"Am I?" Lilly's mouth went dry, and she dropped Marjorie's hands as if they were ice. "I'm just embarrassed, that's all."

Marjorie stepped away from her, her eyes skimming her in one quick sweep. "Right."

Marjorie's mistrust felt like a slap. She winced and wanted to argue, but for a moment, in her friend's suspicious eyes, she saw the truth. Despite the fact she'd rejected the enemy and turned her back on Heinrick, his sapphire eyes glimmered steadily in her mind. He was far from forgotten.

nine

Lilly headed to a bluff overlooking the Missouri, a nook nestled in the shade of a few now withering maples, to read Reggie's letter. The sun, a salmon-colored ball, bled out along the horizon. As the wind loosened her unkempt braid, a meadowlark sang a tune from the fallow field nearby. The smell of dust and drying leaves urged feelings of fall, although the summer heat spilled perspiration down the back of her cotton dress.

This letter was longer, the writing blocked and smudged in places. Lilly determined to analyze each agonizing detail and truly know the cold he'd described in his last letter. More than that, she hoped to sense they were together somehow, that they could bridge this awful, growing chasm between them.

My Dearest Lilly,

I hope this letter finds you well. It's been two weeks since my last batch of mail, and I have concluded that the mail service has fallen into the hands of ineptitude, as has much of this man's army. Although I am proud to be serving the Red, White, and Blue and can say I know it my Christian duty to protect the ideals of democracy, I am sometimes weakened by the lack of supplies and the ever-worsening conditions. I know, in principle, this is not a result of Pershing's leadership or even of President Wilson. Rather, it is the result of too much war, too little sleep, too few supplies, and, worse yet, too many casualties.

I sit now in a reserve trench. Dawn approaches, long shadows licking the edges of the gully where I sleep, eat, and spend my off days. Others head for a nearby village, where they take refuge in French cafes, taverns, and, I fear, boardinghouses within the arms of French women. But of this I do not know firsthand, of course. I will sit here today and try and sleep on my helmet or on one of the many lice-covered bunks left in the shallow dugouts. Oh, how I loathe lice! I feel them move over me as if my skin is somehow unhappy on my bones and seeks to new habitation. I have been without a bath for so long, I have forgotten the sense of water upon my body. How I long for the Missouri.

I spent the last week on the front lines, in the firing trench, curled in a dugout while the cover trench lobbed shells over my sleepless head. We are awake at night, searching the darkness for, foreign bodies that attempt to cut the barbed wire and murder us in our gopher holes. God has preserved me thus far so I know He must be hearing your prayers. One morning, as the dawn revealed the unlucky, I saw that two of my compatriots had been struck. One was a Brit named Martin and the other a fellow Dakotan from Yankton, who had received so much mail here we dubbed him Lucky Joe. I remembered then a moment of agonized cries and frenzied shelling, like lightning in the sky, and knew a firefight had been waged a mere hundred yards from me. And where was I in that desperate moment? Blinking through the darkness, holding at bay the erratic, armed shadows. I know, Lilly, if I blink too long, one of those shadows will emerge, and then I will be the one to sleep forever, slain in this muddy dugout.

Poor Lucky Joe. He often told me of his parents' small wheat plot and worried about their fate with their crops this year without him. He was their only son.

I will not think about it. I will come home to you and our future. It is for you I fight, you and our God-ordained dreams.

Mother, in her last letter, told me you were among those to help house and feed a group of Wyoming doughboys, headed east in May. My heart was both envious to think of those boys having the advantage of seeing your lovely face and pleased my future bride is so faithful in her outpouring of love and concern. I am proud of you, Lilly-girl, and wrote my mother precisely that in a recent letter.

Is it warm there? Did your lilies bloom this year? I remember how tediously you tended them in years past. How are Bonnie and DJ? Chuck tells me all is well with Olive, and I am glad for him. He carries her picture in his helmet.

The sunlight is upon us, and I hear the clang of the kitchen bell. This morning, perhaps, I will get a hot meal. Please hold on to the promises we made and write to your soldier doing his part at the front.

Yours,
Reggie

Lilly smoothed the letter on her lap, and her throat burned. Fixing her eyes on the streak of orange that scraped against the far bluffs, she fought the image of Reggie lying in a dugout hole, a lone man holding back the German lines. On Sunday, she would say an extra-fervent prayer for his safety. Lilly closed her eyes and searched her heart for any sins that might somehow, through Divine justice, send a bullet into Reggie's hideout. She didn't have to dig far to unearth one. It was painfully clear she must fight every errant, impulsive thought of Heinrick, his jeweled eyes and the way she felt embraced by his smile. She must purge the German from her mind and instead cling to the future Reggie had planned. She must do her part to help Reggie come home alive—tend to her letters and never think of anyone but Reggie again. Ever.

A hawk screamed and soared into the horizon, where it melted into the sunset. Behind her, the wind rustled the drying leaves of the maples. They seemed to sizzle as they shattered and fell. The prairie was drying up. The world was at war. And Lilly's future seemed as fragile as the maple leaves.

❧

Lilly held the reins to a dozing Lucy and patted the horse's soft velvet nose. The Appaloosa's eyes were glassy mirrors, glinting the barely risen sun. She gazed at Lilly and seemed to ask, "What am I doing here?"

Lilly rubbed her hand along the forelock of the twenty-year-old mare. "I don't think this is a great idea, either, old girl. Just be careful and don't go too fast."

Not far off, Lilly caught a different set of instructions delivered by her father to his antsy ten-year-old son. "Ride like the wind, Frankie. Don't let those other cowboys nose in front of you. Keep your eyes straight ahead and remember you're a Clark!" He clamped the boy on the shoulder, and Lilly stifled a giggle as Frankie nearly landed in the dirt.

"I don't know, Donald. . . ." Mrs. Clark pinned her husband with a worried look.

"He'll be fine," he assured her.

Lilly tugged on Frankie's beat-up hat as swung into the saddle. "Behave yourself." She knew he had other plans in mind—another route for the race that might indeed place the youngster at the head of the pack. A piercing gunshot ripped through the morning air. Frankie urged Lucy to the starting line. From Lilly's point of view, Frankie would have a time just getting the horse up the hill out of Mobridge, let alone all the way to the Torgesen T and back. Frankie grinned like a hyena, oblivious to the fact he was the youngest contender. Lucy fought sleep. Then the next shot rang out and the pack exploded. Frankie kicked Lucy, wiggled in his saddle, and plowed his way through the dust churned up by the other horses. The horde had long vanished by the time Frankie disappeared behind the bluffs.

Lilly plopped down on the picnic blanket and watched the sun stretch golden fingers into the first hours of the Independence Day picnic. Two hours later, every rider had returned but Frankie. Mrs. Clark sent her husband furious glances as she squinted toward the north. Lilly fought the urge to betray Frankie's plan to cheat and cut a shortcut across the Clark farm to the Torgesen T. Just when she'd decided to turn him in, he and Lucy appeared on the horizon. As they plodded closer, she noticed two things: He and old Luce were covered to their hips in Missouri mud, and he wasn't alone.

Frankie rode in sporting a sheepish grin, bursting with an obvious story to tell. An exuberant crowd greeted him as if he were a doughboy returning from war. But Lilly's eyes were glued to the cowboy in the wide milky ten-gallon hat and muddy black chaps, who beamed like he'd caught the canary. His blue eyes twinkled, and he pinned them straight on Lilly.

Lilly crossed her arms against her chest, turned to Frankie, and ignored the man she couldn't seem to get rid of.

His father helped Frankie down from Lucy, and his mother wrapped him in a fierce hug. Ed Miller, the race official, pushed through the crowd. He glared at Frankie, and demanded an explanation.

Commanding the crowd like a well-seasoned preacher, Frankie spun a tale of adventure and peril. He glossed over the part where he cheated and focused on the usually free-flowing Missouri tributary he'd attempted to cross during his shortcut to win the race.

"Good Ole Luce fought like a rattler caught by the tail, but the mud sucked her down!" All grins, Frankie described Lucy's battle with the clay only the Missouri could produce. Lilly grimaced as she pictured Lucy slogging about in panic, gluing herself and Frankie to the riverbed.

"I tried to break her free, but finally gave up. There weren't anything I could do but holler," Frankie said. To illustrate, he bellowed loudly over the crowd, which elicited riotous laughter from the other competitors.

"I was just plain lucky this here cowboy was near enough to hear me." Frankie gestured to his hero and grinned in glowing admiration. Heinrick, who had moved with his mount to the fringes of the crowd, kept his head down and tugged on his hat. Lilly's heart moved in pity for him. Obviously, he didn't want to revive any previous memories of his appearance in town. But if any of the folks recognized him, they stayed mute. Frankie continued his saga by describing how Heinrick had wrestled Lucy and Frankie from the grip of the mud with an old bald cottonwood.

When Frankie finished his tale, Ed dressed him down, then clamped him on the shoulder. "I do believe, Son, you win the award for most daring contestant." The crowd erupted in good-natured cheering. Even Lilly's father, who had listened with a frown and pursed lips, gave in to forgiveness and tugged on his son's grimy hat.

The crowd dispersed, and Frankie pulled his father over to meet his hero.

"Thank you," Mr. Clark said to Heinrick as he pumped the German's hand.

Heinrick shrugged. "Glad to help." Lilly noticed the proud, triumphant smile had vanished, and in his eyes lurked that lonely, desperate look she'd seen earlier.

"Would you like to stick around for some breakfast? My wife's fixed up some hotcakes and has some homemade peach preserves in her basket."

Lilly's heart jumped. She heard Olive's quick intake of breath behind her. Heinrick looked past her father to Lilly, reaching out to her with his blue eyes and holding her in their magical grip. His tanned face was clean-shaven this morning, although his hair was longer, curling around his ears and brushing the collar of his red cotton shirt. He shifted in his saddle, considering her father's request, all the time staring at Lilly, who felt herself blush. She forced herself to close her eyes and look away.

When she opened them, Heinrick was shaking his head and extending his hand again to her father.

"Thank you, Sir. But I'm afraid I need to prepare for the rodeo this evening, and I don't have time."

Mr. Clark nodded. "I can understand that well enough, Son. Maybe another time."

"Sounds good," Heinrick returned, a smile pushing at his mouth. He tossed a last glance at Lilly, one eyebrow cocked, and an inscrutable, almost teasing look, pulsed in his eyes. Lilly gasped, and the blood simmered in her veins. The nerve of him, suggesting she was wrong and he could be accepted as a friend into their family! Well, her father didn't know he was shaking hands with a German in front of the entire town. Lilly shot Heinrick a halfhearted glare. To her chagrin, Heinrick only gave her a delighted smile. Then he pulled on his hat again, spurred his quarter horse, and trotted toward the Torgesen T.

"Who was that?" gasped Bonnie, her eyes saucers.

Lilly produced an exaggerated shrug, turned away, and pulled Chris from Olive's arms. Olive's dark eyes smoldered. Lilly offered an innocent smile. She'd done nothing to encourage their father's offer, and could she help it if Heinrick had been the only cowboy willing to lend a hand to a scared ten-year-old boy?

Heinrick's comment puzzled her, however. He couldn't possibly be riding in the rodeo, could he? Certainly, Mrs. Torgesen and Clive wouldn't allow him off the ranch to share their little secret. She still hadn't figured out how he'd come to work for them in the first place. But she would never know, because she would never ask.

❧

The blistering sun was on its downward slide, and the heat was dissipating. Still, sheltered in a merciful trace of shade next to the Clark wagon, little Chris's downy curls were plastered to his head in a cap of sweat as he nestled against Lilly. She'd spent the last hour watching her nephew sleep and harnessing her relentless obsession with the mysterious German. Thankfully, thinking upon the events of the fair gave her some respite.

Practically overnight, their little town had become a metropolis, including a fine display of motorized vehicles and parasol-toting French prairie ladies. Their stylish outfits seemed outlandish, however, among the handful of sensible farm wives who wouldn't be caught dead at a picnic in spike-heeled boots and a suit coat. Even so, Lilly and her sisters wore their Sunday best: high-necked blouses, puffy sleeves with lace-trimmed cuffs, and empire-waist cotton skirts. Her mother had even dusted off her wide-brim fedora, saying, "It will keep my face out of the sun."

The picnic started shortly after the race with a weight-guessing contest. Someone suggested they guess the weight of Erica Torgesen, who wasn't there, fortunately, and the townspeople erupted in good-humored laughter. They resorted to guessing the weight of Hans Sheffield's prize burnt-red duroc, and Lilly cheered when Frankie nabbed the prize with a guess of 942 pounds.

Since no one had a scale, they took the word of Hans, who was delighted to hand over the city's prize—free lemonade at Miller's. Frankie and a flock of boys migrated into town and started a stampede that lasted most of the day, until Miller announced he'd run out of juice.

The rest of the picnic continued with an array of harmless amusements from prairie dog chasing to pie eating to rock skipping in the shallow, muddy Missouri. Lilly stayed glued to Olive, watching little Chris and avoiding curious looks from Mobridgites who, she supposed, toyed with the idea she might have been kidnapped. Gratefully, she heard not a scandalous word, and, by the end of the day, Lilly decided the entire event had succumbed to a quiet, merciful death.

"I'm going home now." Olive's lanky shadow loomed over Lilly. "Are you coming with me?"

Lilly considered Chris's sleeping form. His eyes were so gently closed they looked like film. Not a worry lined his face. A small spot of drool moistened her blouse where his lips were propped open and askew. Oh, to be so young, naïve, be gathered inside safe arms and believe the world was in control. "No," Lilly said. "I'm going to the rodeo."

Lilly ignored Olive's vicious glare. She climbed to her feet, eased Chris from her arms, and gently handed him to Olive. Olive marched away, his head bouncing against her bony shoulder.

Lilly beat back the hope of seeing Heinrick and ambled toward the rodeo grounds.

ten

The rodeo grounds teemed with spectators, animals, and anxious cowboys. A pungent brew of dust, animal sweat, hay, and manure hung in the air. The familiarity of it moved a memory in Lilly and she couldn't stop the twinge of guilt. Last year, it had been Reggie she'd come to watch.

Lilly spotted Erica Torgesen perched in all her green finery on the seat of her covered surrey and went to greet her.

"You're looking wonderful tonight, Mrs. Torgesen," Lilly said, grinning.

Mrs. Torgesen winked at her. "You're an angel, Lilly. Already Alpha Booth from Eureka and Eve Whiting have asked for your name. And I gave it to them!" She clasped her hands together, beaming as if she'd just published her best apple pie recipe.

"Thank you," Lilly replied before blending into the swelling crowd. Mrs. Torgesen's reference could mean more business for her, which would in turn help her family. Glancing over her shoulder, she giggled, deciding the eccentric Norwegian resembled a queen upon her throne, peering over her subjects with her little bird in a nest.

Lilly threaded through the crowd to the makeshift bleachers, constructed from dead cottonwood and oak trees dragged from the drying riverbed. Those who didn't want to sit on the skeletons of old trees found stumps or stood on the back of wagons.

Marjorie had commandeered for them a place on the upper branch of a wide peeled cottonwood at the south end of the corral. Lilly climbed aboard next to her friend just in time for the first event. Somehow, the town officials had rounded up more than a smattering of eager cowboys. A group of cowpunchers lined up at the animal pens, adjusting their spurs, straightening their fur chaps, and wiping the sweat from the lining of their Stetsons.

Ed Miller mounted the announcer's platform and yelled over the audience. He read the names of the contestants for the steer wrestling competition. Twenty brave cowboys lined up, and, one by one, young steers were loosed. Lilly's heart beat a race with the hazers as they kept the animals on course. She winced when the bulldoggers ran a steer down on horseback, tackled it, and wrestled the hapless animal to the ground. But the animals pounced to their feet, unscathed.

Occasionally, she broke her attention to search the stands for Heinrick. He was nowhere to be found.

The bulldoggers worked quickly, and a cowpoke named Lou out of Pierre took first prize. Calf roping was next, and another set of unlucky creatures ran through the gamut. Two cowboys from Rapid City won the ten-dollar prize. Sandwiched between events, a clown, Ernestine's Willard, entertained the crowd with cornball antics. His real job was to protect the cowboys from dangerous, enraged animals. Lilly decided he was the perfect clown.

Frankie claimed fifth place in the youth barrel racing event on an exhausted Lucy.

The grand finale was bronco riding, and Lilly was shocked to hear Clive Torgesen's name announced as a contender.

"I saw him bucked off a mustang just last week," she whispered into Marjorie's ear. Marjorie arched her brows in astonishment. Lilly knew Clive's bragging often left an entirely different impression, so she nodded and returned a grim look.

From Ed Miller's introduction, Lilly found out that Clive's bronc, dubbed Jester, had a habit of slamming his body into the fence, squashing his rider's legs. Lilly leaned forward on the branch and held her breath, suddenly thankful for Willard.

The bronc tore out of its pen like a frenzied bee, furious and craving blood. Clive made a valiant show and stayed on for five entire seconds. When Jester finally threw him, he hung in the air, as if taking flight upon a hot gust of wind, and the crowd held their breath in a collective gasp. When he hit the ground, Lilly heard his breath whoosh out as clearly as if he'd landed in her lap. The stands quieted while Willard raced after the bronco and quickly succeeded in snaring his loose reins. He pulled the skittering beast through the exit gate, then rushed to Clive.

Clive rose feebly to his elbows, and it seemed all of South Dakota erupted in a massive cheer. Even Lilly clapped, wondering how he'd managed to stay on that bronco.

The prize went to a fresh young cowpoke from Minnesota, Patrick Hanson. A congregational murmur of appreciation ascended from the stands. The rodeo had managed a decent showing.

Disappointment flickered briefly in Lilly's heart. She doused it quickly, disgusted that she'd wanted to see Heinrick at all, let alone see him perform in a rodeo. But why had he lied to her father?

Ed Miller shot a rifle in the air, the sound creating a cascade of unhappy responses from nearby livestock, as well as mothers with sleeping babes. He held up his arms, and the crowd settled into expectant silence.

"Stick around, folks, we have a new event this evening! Fresh from Wyoming, where cowboys know how to ride the wind, comes—bull riding! This Brahma bull will make your blood curdle! One look at this beast will remind you why cowboys don't ride bulls. We've even found three courageous cowpokes who will give it a go! Please welcome Lou Whitmore from Pierre, Arnie Black from the Double U, and Henry Zook from the Torgesen T!"

Lilly's heart went dead in her chest. It couldn't be. "Heinrick," she whispered.

Marjorie shot Lilly a quizzical look.

Lilly sought out Erica Torgesen's face in the crowd. The woman smiled and chatted with her neighbors, unaffected. Something wasn't quite right. Maybe it wasn't Heinrick. . . .

Then, there he was, on the platform, next to Lou and Arnie, waving his hand to the crowd, his crooked grin flavoring his face with amusement.

What was Heinrick thinking? Those bulls had horns—sharp ones!

"Is that *your* Heinrick?" Marjorie breathed into her ear.

"He's not my Heinrick," Lilly hissed.

"Of course he's not," Marjorie said indignantly. "You know what I mean."

Lilly bit her lip and nodded slowly.

"He's got spunk," said Marjorie in amazement.

"He's going to kill himself," Lilly replied, horrified.

❧

Lou from Pierre sailed through the air. He landed with a grunt and scrambled to his feet. The bull raced after him like a dog to a bone. He swung his massive head, slashing the air, and missed skewering Lou by a hair as the bull rider dove under the fence. The Brahma's bulky frame thudded against the corral. The wood cracked, the sound like a whip, stinging the crowd and extracting a chorus of gasps from terrified women and children. Marjorie covered her mouth with her hands and went ashen. Lilly clenched her fists in her lap.

Having dispatched Lou, the bull turned and memorized the horror-struck crowd, as if searching for his next victim. His black eyes bulged, furious. He breathed in great hot gusts. Fear took control of Lilly's heartbeat. Heinrick was a greenhorn, a laborer from Europe, big but inexperienced. He would be, in a word, sausage. He was either a fool or the bravest man she'd ever met.

Arnie Black from the Double U fared worse than Lou. He escaped the bull's razor-sharp horns only because Willard the Clown rolled a tall rain barrel in his direction. Arnie dove in a second before the bull grazed the backside of his britches. The Brahma rammed the barrel around the corral until it lodged under the bottom of a flimsy fence rail. Arnie scrambled out, breathing hard.

Willard, turning out to be a braver man than Lilly assumed, opened the exit gate and flagged the bull through where three cowpunchers herded him into the starting pen.

Heinrick straddled the pen, one leg on each side of the narrow stall. When ready, he would wind his hand under the rope that encircled the bull's massive body and jump aboard. Lilly held her breath. Heinrick rolled up his sleeve, worked his ten-gallon down on his head, and tugged on his leather glove. His face was grim, his mouth set, and he didn't spare a glance at the crowd. After an eternal moment, he slipped his hand under the belt and nodded. Lilly's heart skidded to a stop.

The bull shot out of the pen, snorting, heaving his body as if possessed. His powerful back legs kicked; he threw himself forward, jerked his head from side to side, whirled and twisted. The stunned crowd was so silent, Lilly could hear Heinrick grunt as the bull jolted him. But he hung on. Five seconds, six. The disbelieving crowd began to murmur. Then the Brahma started to spin, a frenzied cyclone of fury. Lilly covered her mouth to seal her horror. How would Heinrick stay on for the required eight seconds? He would whistle off like a piece of lint, and the bull's horns would spear him on takeoff. Lilly squeezed her eyes shut, then forced them open.

Willard grabbed a red handkerchief and readied himself to dash into the ring.

Suddenly, Heinrick freed a war whoop that sounded like a forgotten echo from the valley of the Little Bighorn. He flung his hand up over his head and rode the bull, melding into the whirlwind spin. Man and beast seemed to flow and dance as if they were one.

A nervous titter rippled through the audience.

Round and round the pair twirled. Lilly lost count of the turns and only watched, mesmerized. Heinrick's powerful legs gripped the sides of the bull and his hat flew off, his blond hair a tangled mass flopping about his head. Lilly could see the muscles ripple through his wide forearm, steady and taut as he clung to the belt. The violence of the event made her reel, yet the raw courage that it took to wrestle a two-ton beast awed her.

A shot fired, and Lilly nearly bolted from her skin. The eight-second mark! Heinrick spurred the bull, and the Brahma burst out of his erratic dance into a headlong stampede for the fence, bucking forward and back. A dusty hazer on a quarter horse shot up to the animal. Heinrick let go of the bull's belt, wrapped an arm around the waist of the cowboy, and slid off his perch. The bull snorted and bolted toward Heinrick. Heinrick hit the ground running and dove under the corral fence. The barrier stopped the Brahma, but as he pawed the dirt, his furious snorts pursued the escaping bulldogger. Willard whooped and sprang into the middle of the ring. The bull turned, considered, and then launched himself toward the next available prey. Willard's quick dash to the exit fence drew the animal like a magnet, and in a moment, he'd dispatched the bewildered bull into a safe holding paddock.

The crowd paused for a well-earned sigh of relief, then exploded in triumph. Henry Zook, whoever he was, was some sort of cowpuncher to last over eight agonizing seconds on a raging bull! Lilly's heart restarted in her chest. She trembled, blew out long breaths, and smoothed the wrinkles from her skirt. Heinrick was a strange brew of interesting surprises, at the very least.

Lilly watched the handsome blond German dust off his coal black chaps and climb the announcer's platform, embedded in riotous applause. Clive Torgesen followed him, waving to the crowd as if he himself had ridden the bull. Lilly's eyes narrowed. What was Clive up to?

Heinrick accepted the handshake and congratulations of a flabbergasted, but beaming Ed Miller. Clive Torgesen stood beside his hired hand, grinning like a Cheshire cat. Ed Miller raised his arms and calmed the crowd.

"Ladies and gentlemen, I am pleased to announce the winner of the first annual Mobridge bull riding contest—Henry Zook, from the Torgesen T!" The crowd burst into another chorus of applause that could have been mistaken for thunder roaring across the prairie. Then, as Ed handed the envelope containing the fifty-dollar prize money to Heinrick, Clive reached over and plucked it from Heinrick's grasp. The clapping died to a spattering.

"And, on behalf of Henry, who represented the Torgesen T in this momentous event, the Torgesen family accepts this award!" Clive waved the envelope above his head, and Lilly noticed Heinrick inhale deeply, his barrel chest rising. But the ever-present white smile never lost its brightness. The crowd offered a modicum of confused applause which quickly died into a raucous murmuring as Clive thumped down the platform steps.

Lilly gaped in bewilderment. Why would Heinrick risk his life, then hand over the prize money—a half-year's salary for a cowhand—? It didn't make sense at all. Heinrick Zook was a confusing tangle of secrets, and he intrigued her more than she wanted to admit.

eleven

Long shadows crawled over the rodeo grounds. Lilly threaded through small clumps of townspeople absorbed in conversation. A sense of reluctance to abandon the illusive normalcy the rodeo, picnic, and fair provided hung heavy in the air.

Lilly was oblivious to the cheerful conversation. Heinrick and his perplexing behavior consumed her mind to the point of distraction. She meandered toward the cattle pens and stopped at the bullpen, where the Brahma raised its head and considered her. A thick rope was tightly knotted around his nose ring, and his wide sides moved in and out in largo rhythm. His eyes were fathomless black orbs, as if he, too, was trying to comprehend the evening's events.

Why did Heinrick give up his painfully-earned prize money for a family who loathed him? She turned over the question in her head, examining it from every angle, discovering nothing.

Gooseflesh prickled her skin a second before clammy breath lathered the back of her neck. Lilly whirled. The pithy odor of whiskey hit her like a fist.

"Well, Miss Lilly. What are you doing over here, staring at the cattle?"

Lilly reeled as Clive Torgesen grabbed the rail behind her. His eyes were dark and swam with trouble.

Fear pounded an erratic beat in Lilly's heart. "Get away from me, Clive." She started to slide away.

Clive snaked out a hand and grabbed her by her slender arm. "Where are you going, Lilly?"

Lilly trembled, and her pulse roared like a waterfall in her ears. Her voice seemed but a trickle behind it. "Let go of me."

"You're such a pretty thing, Lilly. Don't think I haven't

noticed over the years."

Lilly twisted and pulled her arm, but his grip tightened. A cold fist closed over her heart.

"Why, Lilly, it seems to me you should show your boss a little respect."

"You're not my boss," she bit out.

Clive laughed at her. "Sure I am, Honey. You work for the Torgesen T." He leaned close, his unshaven chin scraping her cheek. "And that means you work for me."

Lilly bit her lip. Her knees went weak. "Let me go, Clive."

The smell of dust and sweat enclosed her, and dread pooled in Lilly's throat. She felt a scream gathering, but for some reason couldn't force it out.

Clive's whiskey breath was in her ear. "You know, Lilly, your boy Reggie ain't comin' back. Those Germans are going to kill him like a dog in the dirt, and then you'll need somebody to turn to." He loosed a savage chuckle. "I'm here for you, Darling."

He raised his gloved hand, as if to stroke her cheek. Lilly glimpsed something odious prowling in his dark eyes. Fear shot through her; she lashed out, kicked him hard on the shin.

He swore, caught her other arm, and shook her. "Be nice!"

Lilly glanced over Clive's shoulder. *Please, God, anyone!* But the shadows had widened, and darkness layered the rodeo grounds. Along the bluff, campfires teased her with their safe glow.

"I'm going to scream, Clive."

"Go ahead, Lilly," Clive mocked her. "Who's gonna hear you?"

Lilly trembled as her courage fled. Tears blinded her.

"I will, Clive."

The voice came out of the darkness, with just enough accent for Lilly to recognize it at once.

"Let her go."

A smile curved up Clive's cheek. His eyes narrowed. "I'll be back," he promised as he shoved Lilly against the fence. He whirled. "Get outta here. This ain't none of your business." The curse that followed made Lilly sick. She shrank back, rubbing her arms, poised to bolt as soon as Clive was out of reach.

"What's wrong with you?" Heinrick's disgust thickened his voice, even through the haze of a German accent.

He stepped up to Lilly and held out his hand. "C'mon, Miss." Clive slapped it down. "I said get outta here! Or you'll spend two more years hauling manure on the Torgesen T!"

Heinrick's voice was low, but Lilly detected a warning edge. "I paid you six months' worth tonight, Clive. Christmas, then I'm free. No longer than Christmas."

"We'll see about that." Clive shuffled closer and balled up his fist. The pungent odor of whiskey sauced the air.

Lilly knew she should run, but she couldn't move past the fear that had her rooted.

Heinrick sucked a deep breath, and his voice escaped with a sigh. "You're drunk, Clive. Go home."

"I'm going to skin you like a piece of Missouri driftwood," Clive sneered, undaunted.

A muscle tensed in Heinrick's jaw, but he blinked not an eye as he batted away Clive's fist. Clive roared and charged, throwing his arms around Heinrick's waist. The German stepped back and easily tossed Clive to the ground. Clive wobbled to his knees and wheezed.

Lilly's fingers bit into her arms as she waited for Heinrick to resign Clive, face first, to the dirt. Instead, Heinrick swiped Clive's fallen Stetson from the ground and held it out. "Go home, Mr. Torgesen. It's late, and you're tired."

Clive cranked his head upward and glared at Heinrick, his brown hair matted, a line of drool dangling from his lips. He leaned back on his haunches and lunged for his hat, snaring, instead, Heinrick's forearm. He yanked hard and landed a blow on the German's cheek. It echoed like the snap of an old cottonwood.

Heinrick jerked back. He set his jaw, and his eyes hardened to ice. His fists balled, but he held them to his sides.

"Okay, that's enough. Go home, Boss."

The exertion of that one punch had emptied Clive. He gaped at Heinrick, his mouth askew, confusion glazing his eyes.

Heinrick stepped toward Lilly and again extended his hand. She hesitated, then slid hers into it. His hand was warm and firm and held hers with gentleness. Lilly scooted around Clive like a jittery cat.

Lilly and Heinrick marched ten quick, solid paces before he released her hand. It continued to tingle, and she felt the absence well. Heinrick had saved her. The significance of that hit her hard, and she squinted at the man she'd considered her enemy.

"I never did get your name," Heinrick said, his eyes ahead.

Lilly fought a war of emotions. He was still a foreigner, the enemy. But as she walked next to him, hearing only the crunch of prairie grass and the beating of her heart, she knew that wasn't a fair assessment. He deserved courtesy, if not her friendship. "Lillian," she whispered. "But my friends call me Lilly."

"Lilly it is, then." A smile tugged at his lips.

They walked through the velvet darkness, the field grass crunching under their steps, the crickets singing from the riverbed not far off, and a lazy ballad humming over the bluffs from distant campfires. The wind skimmed the aroma from a pot of stew and carried it across the prairie. Lilly's stomach flopped, but not from hunger.

"I guess I owe you." She peeked at Heinrick and saw his smile widen.

"How's that?"

"You're one up on me. You saved Frankie and now me."

Heinrick chuckled, and Lilly was oddly delighted.

"Well, let me see. How can you save me?"

Lilly walked along and pondered that question, wondering what she could offer a man who seemed to carry the world in his wide palms, wondering even if she should. Curiosity swelled inside her. Who was this man, and why did he risk everything for the Torgesen T? The confusion stopped her short.

Heinrick walked out before her.

"Heinrick?"

He turned. "I haven't heard anyone use my name for nearly five years. It sounds like a song coming from your lips."

Lilly's delight was like a strong gust of warm wind. She felt an impending blush and bit her lip. But the endearing twinkle in his eyes mustered her courage. "Why did you give Clive your prize money?"

His expression darkened.

"What is it?" Lilly's heart fell, afraid she'd offended him after he'd been so kind to her. "I'm sorry."

Heinrick held up a hand to stave off her apology. He gazed into the protective obscurity of night. "I gave Clive the money because," he cleared his throat but couldn't dislodge a distinct hoarseness, "they own me."

"What? How can they own you?"

Heinrick freed a sigh of pure frustration. "It's a long story, Lilly."

She crossed her arms. "I like stories."

Heinrick winced as if his words brought pain. "I don't think that is a good idea."

He turned away, running a hand through his thick, curly hair. "Don't you remember? I'm the enemy. Your fiancé, Reggie, is being killed by my relatives." He blew out another breath, then turned back to her. "I'm dangerous."

A brief, melancholy smile flickered over his face, but his eyes betrayed ache. "Or did you forget?"

Shame poured over Lilly. He was right, and the truth of it distanced them as if he was a coyote and she a long-eared jackrabbit. They were enemies.

Somehow, however, Lilly just couldn't muster up the feelings of loathing one ought to feel for an enemy. Today had changed all that. He'd gone out of his way to save Frankie and had toed up to Clive for her. Heinrick was too kind, too forgiving, too, well, downright honorable to be the enemy. And therein lay the paradox. She didn't want him to be an enemy. She wanted him to be Heinrick, her friend. It would mean nothing. Reggie was still her fiancé. She wasn't stepping past the boundaries of their covenant.

Heinrick wasn't part of the massacre. He was, in fact, a casualty himself, imprisoned and wounded by Clive and the Torgesen T. And he needed a friend. If Reggie were caught behind German lines, hurt and friendless, wouldn't she want some kind German *fraulein* to watch over him? The answer sealed her decision.

"You're not my enemy, Heinrick. I was wrong to call you that. Please forgive me."

His radiant smile nearly knocked her off her feet. "You're forgiven." His reply lit a glow of peace in Lilly's heart.

"Please," she said softly, "tell me your story."

Heinrick's eyes crinkled with delight. They turned and began to stroll across a prairie lit only by the windows of heaven and an unblemished full moon.

"Well, the Lord sure does bless a man when he is patient. To think my first friend in this new country is a pretty little lady named after a flower."

Lilly caught her breath, ignored the trembling of her heart, and slowly relaxed into the gentle rhythm of his step.

twelve

Heinrick unfurled his story as they strolled into the black expanse of prairie. With each step, Lilly sensed that the telling was a catharsis, a long healing sigh after years of silence. The soft strength of his voice soon erased her haunting encounter with Clive.

"I was born in Germany, but my mother, Anna, was Norwegian. She came to Germany to study and lived in Hullhorst. My father worked as a farm hand in Neidringhausen, a nearby village." Heinrick swiped off his hat and rubbed the rim as he walked.

"As love stories go, Papa met her at a church social and they were married a few months later. My best memory of Mama is watching her roll out the *kuchen* in our tiny kitchen. She always gave me the first piece, sprinkled with sugar." He hummed. "I love the taste of a freshly fried roll *kuchen*." He paused, and she felt memory in his tone. "Mama was laughter and sunshine, sugar, kisses, and the smell of fresh bread." He paused again, this time longer. "I was eight when she died of typhoid fever."

Lilly bowed her head. "I'm sorry."

"My father never recovered," he said hoarsely. "To an eight year old, a father's despair can be felt as your own. I suppose I was really a. . .what do you call a person without parents?"

"An orphan."

"*Ja*, an orphan. My mother had family in Norway and distant cousins in America. They arranged passage when I was seventeen, five years ago. I've spent one year working for each family, paying off my passage." Heinrick's voice turned hard. "And then some."

The wind fingered the disobedient strands of Lilly's hair,

tickling her neck. "So, the Torgesens *do* own you."

Heinrick sighed. He stopped and turned, his face a defined shadow in the darkness. "No, I was wrong to say that. The Torgesens don't own me. I came to America of my own will, and I chose to honor my promise, or rather my family's promise, to them. Perhaps they consider me their servant, but I serve them because I serve my Lord."

"Your Lord?"

"God Almighty, the Maker of the heavens and the earth."

Lilly nodded. "Of course. I am a Christian."

Joy glittered in Heinrick's eyes. "So am I!"

Lilly frowned. "How can you be—?"

"Just because I am German doesn't mean I don't love and worship the same Jesus you do. Not all German Christians agree with Kaiser Bill. But we do agree the Lord Jesus is God and our hope for eternal life."

Lilly frowned. She hadn't considered that a foreigner, especially a German, would know the same God she did. She felt a strange kinship with this foreigner. "What will you do when your debt is paid?"

They began to walk again, bumping now and then when the prairie knocked them off balance.

"I don't know. Whatever God tells me to do, I suppose."

"Don't you have a plan? A dream?"

The breeze juggled Heinrick's laughter. "I have many dreams, Lilly. A family, a home, a good job, but most of all I dream of serving the Lord, wherever He desires to put me."

"How will you know? Who will tell you where that is?"

"God will, of course." Heinrick stopped, turned to her. "Doesn't God tell you what He wants you to do?"

Lilly stared past him, out into the sky, into the eternity where her God lived. "He doesn't have to. I already know."

Heinrick arched his brows.

"I'm going to marry Reggie when he comes home and be a pastor's wife. We have it all planned out."

"Who has it planned?" Heinrick said softly.

Lilly shivered. He wasn't just looking at her, he looked *into* her, examining her soul. The prairie was suddenly small, the night sky enclosing, the breeze cold, his presence invasive, and their walk, reckless.

The whinny of a horse shot through Lilly like an arrow. She whirled, squinted through the darkness, and recognized her father astride old Lucy. Frankie snoozed on Lucy's neck.

"I have to go," Lilly said quietly.

Heinrick nodded. He crossed his hands over his chest. Lilly stepped away, a tentative, grateful smile pushing at the corners of her mouth.

"Thank you for saving me, Heinrick."

Something in his eyes made her hesitate and halt her dash to intercept Frankie and her father. Standing there, with his shoulders sagging and with the wind shifting his golden mass of hair, Heinrick appeared every inch the orphan he'd described earlier. His eyes reached out to her with an almost tangible longing.

"Lilly, wait." Heinrick cupped a hand behind his neck and examined his scuffed boots. "You *can* save me back."

Lilly's eyes widened. "How?" She could hear Lucy scuffing closer.

"Teach me to read."

"What?"

"Teach me to read English. I never learned, and I'd like to be able to read and write."

Lilly glanced at her father. He hadn't seen them yet. Teach Heinrick to read? That would mean spending time with him, getting to know him.

It was a bad idea. She knew it in her heart. Her father may have been friendly this morning, extending the hand of fellowship to Heinrick when he thought him a ranch hand and Frankie's hero. But eventually he would find out he was German. . .then what? And what about Reggie? He could never know.

But Heinrick had called her a blessing. And he'd risked his

freedom for her, standing up to Clive Torgesen. She owed him.

"Okay, one lesson, to teach you the alphabet. Agreed?"

He resembled a schoolboy with his churlish grin. "When?"

Her father was nearly within earshot. "Tomorrow, in the maple grove on the bluff near our property. Do you know where?"

Heinrick nodded.

"After church."

"I'll be there."

Lilly slipped into the envelope of darkness, heading toward Frankie and her father. The wind stirred the prairie grass, and Lilly thought she heard Heinrick call after her, *"Auf Wiedersehen,* Lilly."

thirteen

The condemnation that simmered in her chest during the morning worship service, under the glare of Rev. Larsen's stern sermon, threatened to turn her away from her promise. Then her mother had to ask her where she was off to when she breezed past her on the way to the maple glen.

"Going down to the river," Lilly answered, but shame settled upon her and deceit felt like a scarlet letter around her neck, even if based on the best of intentions. If Reggie found out, he would be cut to the core. At best, it would be hard to explain. At worst, he would leave her at the altar, resigning her to spinsterhood. She could be annihilating her dreams by this one simple meeting.

But the mystery of her German friend was just too puzzling to ignore. Since the day his mustang had almost plowed over her, Heinrick had been chipping his way into her thoughts. Her mind kept returning to a moon-basked prairie and the memory of a tall, muscled German disappearing into the folds of darkness. Heinrick's low, gentle voice, the syllables of foreign words, and his heart-filling laughter dulled her pangs of guilt. Moreover, Heinrick was a walking contradiction. There was something about him that seemed peaceful, unencumbered, even free. Yet he wasn't free. He was, for all practical purposes, an indentured servant, paying off a bill that seemed way too high. And he counted it as serving the Lord. He seemed even joyous about the task, and Lilly couldn't unravel the paradox in that. Bondage was not joyous. It was suffocating.

In the end, this riddle drove her to the river.

❧

The maple glade had skimmed an adequate supply of cool air

from the morning, and gooseflesh rose on Lilly's arms as she entered the shaded glen. A ripe river scent, rich in catfish and mud, rode in on the breeze and threaded through the trees. Lilly shoved a few rebellious, damp strands of hair under her hat, rubbed her arms, and hunted for her pupil.

He wasn't there. Lilly listened to the wind hiss through the leaves, feeling uneasy. Maybe it was for the best. She half-turned, poised to fly back to the farm and blot Heinrick from her memory, when he emerged from the shadows.

He peered at her with curious eyes and a crooked smile. "*Guten tag.*"

He'd dressed for the occasion: a clean pair of black trousers, polished ebony cowboy boots, a fire-red cotton shirt, and a buckskin vest. His blond hair may have been neatly combed, but the wind had laughed at his efforts and mussed it into wild curls. A hint of blond stubble peeked from tanned cheeks.

"You're here." Lilly gulped.

"Of course," he said. "I wouldn't miss it."

"Ready for school?" Lilly's voice sounded steadier than she felt. She shuffled toward him, dead leaves crunching beneath her boots.

He cocked his head, and a hint of mischief glinted in his blue eyes. "I'm not a very good student."

Nervousness rippled up Lilly's spine and spread out in a tingle over her body. Then Heinrick grinned wide and white, and his smile encircled her like an embrace. She had to admit he was just plain charming. She bit her lip and looked away, lest he see something he ought not to in her eyes.

His smile dimmed. "What is it, Lilly? Do you still think I'm the enemy?"

Lilly hid her eyes, staring at her shoes. "No, it's not that." Her mind raced. "I just don't know if I can help you. . . ."

Heinrick slid a hand under her elbow, and Lilly almost flew out of her skin. "I think you can help me more than you know."

The soft tone of his voice brought her gaze to his face. His eyes pleaded with her, and the longing in them took her breath away. "Please?" he whispered.

Since her mouth was dry and wordless, Lilly nodded.

"Let's sit by the river."

Heinrick led her into the sunshine, down the bluff, and they sat on a piece of bald cottonwood. Lilly pulled out her Bible, and passed it to him.

He held it in his large, rough hands and caressed the smooth leather with his thumbs. "A Bible," he murmured.

"Do you have one?"

"Of course, although mine is in German."

She nodded, letting that information digest. Then she flipped the Bible to Genesis. and read the first verse. "Reading is just a matter of decoding the letters, sounding them out to form words your ear already knows."

"My ear doesn't know many words."

"Heinrick, I've heard enough to know that you will read just fine. You have a wonderful vocabulary. And what words you don't know, I'll explain."

He nodded, and she continued the lesson. "Our English alphabet is made up of twenty-six letters. From these letters, you form words, using a few basic rules, which I will teach you. First, let's learn the letters."

She pointed out each letter from the text in Genesis. He was a good student, despite his warning, turning each one over his tongue with little accent. Recognition came more quickly than she expected, and by the time the bluff swathed them in shadow, he'd read all the words in the first and second verses.

Lilly beamed at him. "You're a good student."

"Thanks," he said, his gaze buried in the Bible. He was running his finger over the third verse when she pulled the book from his grasp and folded it on her lap.

"Enough school," she declared. "Tell me why I've never met you before. I've been working for Erica Torgesen for almost a year."

"I only just arrived to the Torgesens. I've lived many

places in America: New York City, Ohio, Milwaukee, Iowa, and now Dakota."

He acted as if it was normal to live so many places, like a homeless stray.

"I see," Lilly said, realizing how lonely his life must be. "Do you miss your home?"

He was silent, and when he turned to her, a thousand images gathered in his eyes. He blinked as if trying to get a fix on just one. Then the images dissolved, leaving a residue of pain in their wake. "Yes."

Lilly noticed how his hands curled over his knees, completely encasing them.

"But Germany isn't home anymore."

Lilly's eyebrows gathered her confusion.

"Dakota is home now. I am home wherever God puts me, because I am in God's hands."

Lilly shook her head. "Home is family. Home is friends. God gives us those, but you certainly can't say that Reggie, or Chuck, or Harley are home."

"Perhaps. But to spend your entire life yearning for something else, instead of surrendering to God's plans seems like a foreign land to me. Home is peace. And peace is being where God puts you."

"And God has put you here, in bondage to the Torgesens?"

"For now. But I know He has a plan, just like He had a plan for Joseph in the book of Genesis. I just have to trust Him and wait."

"But what if. . . ?" The words lodged in her throat. She looked downstream, away from Heinrick.

"What if what, Lilly?"

"What if things get messed up; what if life doesn't go according to plan?" Lilly felt Heinrick's gaze on her neck and bit her lip. She knew she'd just opened her heart for his scrutiny.

"Whose plan?" he asked softly. His knee bumped hers as he turned toward her.

Lilly swallowed her leaden heart. "Well, our plan, of course.

The plan of life, the one we spend our entire lives creating."

"Whose plan is it, though? Don't you think Joseph struggled over the death of his dreams, while trudging behind a caravan of camels on his way to Egypt? But he trusted God's plans, even while sitting in a prison, accused of a crime he didn't commit. God delivered him and a nation. Shouldn't all our plans belong to God?"

Lilly studied her fingernails, acutely aware of his gaze on her. "But God's plans are what the church and your parents say they are, aren't they? Isn't that God's voice?"

"It could be. God does speak through our church and family." He nodded slowly. "That's one way."

"How else, then, do you know what God wants you to do?"

Heinrick tapped her Bible. "God's Word. You have to read. God's plans are revealed one day at a time, through His Word and the Holy Spirit working in our lives."

Lilly rubbed the leather. "Listen, Heinrick. This is all very interesting, and I am sure, where you come from, it is part of your religion. But here, God leads me through my pastor, through my parents, and through Reggie. I just have to obey them to do what God wants."

Heinrick stared out over the water and beyond. "Lilly, do you know the difference between faith and obedience?"

Lilly's eyes narrowed and she shook her head warily. Whose lesson was this, anyway?

"Why wasn't Cain's sacrifice acceptable to God?"

Lilly frowned, confused. Heinrick's eyes gleamed, so intent was he on his sermon. He tucked a hand over hers on the Bible.

"Because it was a fruit offering?" she stammered, her gaze on his warm hand.

"No. It wasn't about the offering; it was about his heart. God looked at Cain and Abel first, then upon their offerings. He looked at their hearts and their faith. Cain's offering was all about fulfilling the law, about serving himself, about doing what was necessary to secure his forgiveness. But Abel's heart belonged to God, and he offered his lamb out of worship and faith in God's salvation. Abel's sacrifice was accepted because of his faith."

"Lilly, faith is an action. Obedience is a reaction. We obey God because we love Him, not because we want God to love us or want to earn a place in heaven."

Lilly lifted her chin. "Show me your faith, and I will show you my faith with actions."

Heinrick pulled the Bible from her hands and flipped through it. Silently he scanned the pages, then, blowing out a breath, he handed it back to her. "Could you read Hebrews 11:1 for me, please?"

She scowled at him, but found it and read aloud, "'Now faith is the substance of things hoped for, the evidence of things not seen.'" Lilly closed the Bible.

"'If you love me you will obey my commands,'" she countered. She hadn't spent years softening a pew for nothing.

Heinrick sighed and again pulled God's Word from her lap. He flipped, wearing his determination like a mask. But, in time, his resonant tenor voice stammered out the verse. "For by grace are ye saved through faith; and that not of yourselves: it is the gift of God: Not of works, lest any man should boast.'" He paused. Lilly listened to the hammering of her heart.

When he at last spoke, the words seemed to unroll from his very soul, passionate, authentic, and nearly desperate.

"Lilly, God loves us so much that when we were still sinners, before we obeyed even His slightest desire, He died for us. We don't have to earn His love or His salvation. He has good things waiting for us, even if sometimes it doesn't seem like it. We have to be like Joseph. He put his life into God's hands on a daily, moment-by-moment basis. But to put your life into God's hands and to surrender to His plans, you need to know Him. You have to read the Bible to know what He wants you to do."

"I know the Bible. It says that faith is obedience."

"Obedience is evidence of faith, Lilly. It isn't faith itself. Faith is unwavering trust in God to lead and to guide, wherever He wants. And it is knowing, in the pit of your soul, that He loves you and knows best."

His eyes glowed with their intensity. She wanted to flinch, but his gaze drew her in, like a warm fire on a cold night. Heinrick passed her the Bible. "Hebrews 11:6."

No one had ever spoken to her this way, not Rev. Larsen and certainly not Reggie. It seemed edging near impropriety to be talking about God so openly, so intimately with anyone, let alone Heinrick. Yet she was drawn to the mystery of his God, and when she read the words, something seemed to ignite deep inside her.

"'But without faith it is impossible to please him: for he that cometh to God must believe that he is, and that he is a rewarder of them that diligently seek him.'"

Lilly closed the Bible and rubbed the smooth leather.

"Lilly," Heinrick whispered, "do you have faith in God? Do you trust Him to plan and manage your life on His terms? Do you know He loves you?"

Lilly bit the inside of her lip to keep tears at bay. "I'm confused. I don't know God that well, maybe."

Heinrick's voice was soft, like a caress on her skin, yet his words still bruised. "Lilly, perhaps you're afraid. Do you think that if you knew God and heard His voice, He might tell you something you don't want to hear?"

Lilly swiped away a tear.

The sun polished the surface of the river platinum. "I need to get home," Lilly mumbled.

"And I have chores," Heinrick agreed, but his voice betrayed disappointment. He pushed himself from the driftwood, then turned and offered her his hand. Lilly deliberated, then slipped her hand into his.

"Tomorrow?" he asked. "I promise I'll be a good student."

"You were a good student today," she replied, lifting her chin. She stood almost to his shoulder and noticed how the buttons to his shirt pulled slightly across his wide chest. He put an arm around her waist and hauled her to the top of the bluff. They stood there for a moment, the wake of their conversation shifting between them like a fragrance neither could acknowledge.

"Tomorrow, after supper," Lilly blurted. Then she yanked her hand from his and ran toward home.

fourteen

Lilly sat on the bald cottonwood by the river watching the amber sky melt into the mud, listening to the crickets scold her for her naiveté. Why had Heinrick stood her up? After four days, she'd learned to count on his punctuality. He read with remarkable precision, and although she hated to admit it, his accented voice made warm syrup run through her veins. Her heart began to long for that moment when he turned his blue eyes into hers and asked for another lesson.

Where was Heinrick? Tears bit her eyes. How rude! Didn't he know that she dodged suspicion every time she raced down to the river to meet him? It was becoming harder to weave tales that only skimmed the definition of lies.

But she ached to see him. Heinrick was no longer a mystery, an enigma, to her. He'd ended each lesson with a story, something from his childhood. He wanted to own land. To travel. To have a family. And he longed for, more than anything, to find a niche for himself in this new world. He'd left it unspoken, but Lilly guess that Heinrick's deepest fear was his harsh reality—being forever a foreigner in his adopted homeland. She couldn't help feel as if he had handed her the delicate pieces of his heart.

And now that she'd seen it, she was drawn even more to the mysterious German, to his gentle character, his passionate love for God, his simple yet noble dreams.

Was this the end? Was it the end of his infectious laughter, his enthralling stories of an unruly boyhood in the Black Forest? Lilly dug her nails into her bare arms and steeled herself against the ripple of sorrow. How could she expunge the flame that he had ignited in her heart? The warmth of their friendship drew her to the bluff every evening like the glow of a beckoning campfire on a brisk autumn night. Somehow, even the July twilight would seem cold without Heinrick's smile.

Was Heinrick playing games? Maybe all he really wanted from her was language lessons. Had she imagined the warmth in his eyes and the softness of his touch on the small of her back?

A sour brew of fury and hurt burned in her throat. She jumped to her feet and scrambled up the bluff. It was all for the best, anyway. Heinrick was nothing but trouble, and she should have seen that when his horse almost trampled her.

Lilly marched through the grove, her feet pounding out a rhythm with her heart. Tears dripped down her cheek, and she violently whisked them away. She'd been a fool to trust him, to let him into her heart. At least she would be free of his endless probing questions about her faith. His God was simply different from hers. . .closer somehow, but perhaps that wasn't a good thing. She hardly wanted to trust a God who might cast her into the hands of a person like Clive Torgesen. Heinrick must have fallen out of God's favor, somehow, although she questioned the idea of such an honorable man offending God. Still, surely, God blessed those more who obeyed Him best. It just made sense that God balanced things out, and if she managed her side correctly, He would keep things even.

Lilly skidded to a halt in the middle of a withered clump of goldenrod. Maybe this was God's way of punishing her! She'd betrayed Reggie and deserved to have her heart ripped out, even by another man. Shame wound into her soul.

She'd made a terrible mistake. The only thing left to do was to forget. Thankfully, Reggie would be home soon, and the entire horrid experience could be safely tucked inside a secret chapter of her life, never to be read.

Lilly tightened her jaw as she climbed up the porch steps. She tiptoed into the house, noting her mother knitting at the kitchen table, lost in conversation with her father. Lilly ducked her head, scampered up the stairs, and threw herself across the bed. There, in the privacy of her folded arms, she cried herself to sleep.

❧

Her subconscious put a picture to her fears. She found herself on a battlefield, searching among wide-eyed, lifeless soldiers. Some clutched pictures of sweethearts; others embraced their weapons like teddy bears. Lilly whimpered as she peered into faces, finally uncovering the one she feared to find. She cried out when she saw him, his dark hair hanging over his closed eyes, lying upon a pile of erupted earth as if he was sleeping. She crawled to him, gasping, and removed his helmet. His face was covered in a layer of black stubble, and he seemed warm. But she knew, as she curled a hand under his filthy neck, Reggie was dead.

In the background, she heard the *rat-a-tat-tat* of machine gun fire. A voice, crisp and clean and accented in German, rose over the clatter. "Trust me."

Lilly shuddered, for in its wake came a knowledge that if she surrendered, it would cost her everything she held dear, her dreams, her will, her very life.

Lilly woke herself up screaming.

fifteen

Five days crawled by, and the dream, instead of dissolving into the hazy folds of memory, invaded like a virus, multiplying in strength and repeating itself in crisp, horrifying detail every night. Lilly awoke each time gasping, tears rushing down her cheeks, hands clenching the snarled bedclothes. Twice she woke up Bonnie, who frowned with worry in the streams of dawn. Perhaps her sister had even mentioned it, because once, while Lilly and her mother gathered in the sun-dried laundry, her mother questioned Lilly about not sleeping well. Her mother hesitated when Lilly brushed off the matter, but didn't pursue the truth.

Lilly clawed through the days, trying to drown the German-accented voice in her ears. She pulled weeds, the only things that seemed to be thriving in the kitchen garden, canned cucumbers, and stirred jam on the potbellied stove. Not once did she wander down to the river after dinner hour.

On Thursday, Olive returned from Mobridge with two letters, one for herself and the other for Lilly. Olive tucked the letter from Reggie into Lilly's apron pocket while Lilly was wrist deep in a bowl of bread dough. The kitchen smelled of dill weed and onions, and jars of pickles cooled on the washboard. Lilly, shocked at the addition to her apron pocket, glanced at Olive. Her sister returned a glower.

"Did you forget the mail train came today?" Olive balled her hands on her.

Lilly's mouth dropped open, not only at Olive's loaded accusation, but also at the knowledge that she did, indeed, forget about the train and for the briefest of moments, Reggie.

"What is wrong with you?" Olive's screeching voice summoned their mother to the kitchen. "You're stumbling around the house like a drunkard, not paying attention to anyone! Why, yesterday, Alice Larsen came by, and you didn't even come out of your room to greet her." Olive's lip curled and she nearly snarled. "What sort of daughter-in-law are you?"

"That's enough, Olive," her mother said sharply. "Please leave us."

Olive shot an exasperated scowl at her mother, then stormed out of the room.

As Mrs. Clark sat on a straight-backed chair, Lilly dove into her bread dough and kneaded with vigor.

"You *have* been acting strangely, Lilly. I'd call it snippy, and that's not you." She paused and touched Lilly's forearm. "Bonnie told me about the nightmares. Sit, Child, and talk to me."

Dread multiplied through her bones as Lilly met her mother's gaze. But her eyes beheld a tenderness that reached out and enfolded her, and Lilly's fear ebbed. She wiped her hands on her apron and drew up a chair, wondering what to reveal, opting for the truth.

"I taught that cowboy who saved Frankie how to read."

The shock Lilly expected was strangely absent. The older woman folded her hands together on the table. "Hmm, so that's what you were doing."

"You knew?"

Her mother's eyes twinkled. "I know a lot more than you think, Lilly. I watched you every night clean up, fix your hair, and change your dress. I knew it wasn't for the prairie dogs. And, when you finally floated home, I knew something other than the sunset had touched your heart."

"Why didn't you stop me?"

Mrs. Clark studied her clasped hands. "Because I trust you. Obviously more than Olive does. And I know in your heart is a seed of goodness and wisdom."

Lilly blew out a ragged breath. "Does Father know?"

Her mother shook her head. "He's too worried about the wheat and the drought to be caught into the tangled mystery of his daughter's heart." She reached for Lilly's hand. "Darling, this nightmare. Does it have to do with the cowboy?"

Lilly closed her eyes, seeing Heinrick's heart-catching smile and his mesmerizing blue eyes. "Mother, do you pray?"

"Of course."

"No, I mean pray, when you aren't in church. By yourself, without Pastor Larsen leading you."

Her mother smiled. "I pray when I hang laundry, when I see the sunshine spray the grass with tiny gold sparkles. I pray when I kiss DJ and Frankie in their sleep and see the peace of innocence written upon their faces. I pray when I see your father, dozing in his rocking chair, his spectacles dripping down over his nose and the Bible open on his lap. I pray for Olive and Christian and especially Chuck every night when I read the paper. And I pray when I notice you, Lilly, standing at the edge of the yard, your long hair taken by a prairie gust. I thank God and pray for His protection and His will to be done in all our lives."

Her mother's speech enraptured her. For the first time, Lilly considered her mother had thoughts beyond cooking, and canning, and hanging laundry. She saw her mother young, dreaming of a family and a home, and most of all trusting in a God who reigned over her life. In that instant, Lilly was jealous. Jealous her mother knew where she was planted and was already reaping the harvest in the garden of life God had given her.

Somehow, during the past week, Lilly's own surety about the life she thought God had planted for her had been swept up like dry prairie soil into a whirlwind of doubt. Heinrick's suggestion that God would do what He wanted, regardless of her prayers and her sacrificial obedience to everyone's plans for her, scared her more than she would admit. Was Heinrick right? Were she and Reggie like Joseph, helpless and at the mercy of an unpredictable God?

"Mother, did you always know it was God's plan for you to marry Father?"

Mrs. Clark gave a slight frown. "Have I never told you how I met your father?"

"You met him at a social at your church."

Her mother shook her head. "It wasn't at my church. Your father was from a church in the country, a different denomination. And, Lilly, I had promised to marry another man."

Lilly froze.

Her mother nodded. "He was a rich man, had been married before, and his wife died giving birth to their son. But he was still young and a friend of your grandfather's. He wanted a wife, and my father wanted a secure future for his only daughter. So Timothy began to court me. He was a very nice man. Good humored and kind. He treated me with respect, and my family and friends told me it was a good match. And, I agreed. So he proposed to Father, then to me, and the plans were laid."

Lilly's chin drifted downward.

"Then I met your father." A playful smile lit on her mother's face. "He was a hired hand on a farm outside town. I went to the social with my friend, Marcie, whom I was visiting for the weekend. We were studying together at a finishing school in Chicago. Donald was at the social, and the day I met him, I knew."

"You knew?" Lilly breathed.

Her mother's eyes sparkled with an unfamiliar passion. "I knew I couldn't do what was expected, that I couldn't live a life committed to a man I did not wildly love."

"Mother!"

Mrs. Clark sat back in her chair, folding her hands across her chest. "It's true, Lilly. Marriage is difficult and not a place for lukewarm commitment. I knew if I married Timothy, it would be for many good reasons, but not the one that mattered."

"But what about your family, your parents?"

"Your father was patient. He courted me for three years and proved to my parents that he was committed and a hard worker. Finally your grandfather relented."

"But weren't you afraid?"

"I was more afraid of not surrendering to God's plans for my life and missing out, perhaps, on the fullness of joy He wanted for me."

"How did you know that was what God wanted. . .I mean, your father and all your friends said you should marry Timothy. Why wasn't that God's plan?"

"Because I never felt it was right. I knew I didn't truly love Timothy, although he would have been a wonderful husband, I am sure. When I prayed, it seemed as though God wrote your father into my heart. He was the answer."

"So, in answer to your question, yes, marrying your father was always the plan. But I didn't know it until I asked, then listened to God."

Lilly blew out a troubled breath. "Well, I know it is God's plan for me to marry Reggie."

Her mother's chair creaked as she leaned forward. "God always has a plan for our lives, Lilly. But it may not be the one we think it is. We have to ask Him, then listen."

Lilly sloped back in her chair and crossed her arms, not sure she'd recognize God's voice if she heard it.

❧

Dinner was a quiet, contemplative event. Lilly's father informed the family that haying season had arrived, and Olive read portions of Chuck's letter aloud.

We rotate through the line of trenches by week; next week Harley and Reggie and I will move forward to the supply trench, running ammunition to the support trench. I feel most sorry for the Sammies stuck in their bunkers on the front, knowing it's wet and cold and they are eating out of tin cans. But, in two weeks, I will be there, and they will feel sorry for me. Don't worry, Olive, for our good Lord protects us, and in a few short months I'll return, victory in hand. Kiss my Christian for me.

Corporal Charles Wyse

Reggie's letter burned a hole in Lilly's pocket and suddenly she wanted to tear it open, clutch it to her chest, and remind herself of the sanity of their commitment.

Olive's tears streaked down her cheeks, and next to Lilly, Bonnie hiccupped a sob. Melancholy bound them together in silent meditation.

"He'll be back, Olive," Lilly reassured in a solemn tone. Olive lifted red-rimmed eyes, attempting an acquiescing grin. It dissolved into the trembling of her chin. She buried her face in Christian's neck.

Guilt pierced Lilly's heart and twisted. How could she have forgotten Reggie?

Olive wiped her stained cheeks with a free hand. "Lilly, I saw Erica Torgesen at Ernestine's. She asked if you could come to the ranch tomorrow."

Despite the wild dance of her disobedient heart, Lilly bit her lip and nonchalantly nodded.

❧

Lilly stretched across her bed and read Reggie's letter.

Dear Lilly,

I gladly received your letter of June 23, and your tender words greatly encouraged me. I cannot express to you adequately the happiness your promise brings me; it is a beacon of hope during this chaotic and unforgiving war. When the enemy is upon us, shells exploding in our bunkers, I clutch my helmet and think only of you, your emerald eyes, and the future we have laid out. I am not the only doughboy to cling to dreams of home; this hope is the veritable fuel that drives all us good Sammies over the top in a desperate attempt to chase those Germans back into the hole from which they crawled and thereby return to our shores that much sooner.

I am sure you have heard of Harley's proposal to Marjorie. I advised him toward it, he being the shy one. I assured him that Marjorie's promise would give him the courage he needs to survive this horrendous war. Just as you give to me. He is

*happy, and, although he has not received her reply, he is
assured in his heart of her affirmation.*

As I write this, the sun is disappearing behind our lines,
giving relief to the relentless view of the unburied dead,
destroyed machinery, and shattered earth. Tonight I am in a
cover trench, my job to fire over the heads of those in the firing trench as they move along the front. Hopefully we will
not hear, "Over the top!" this evening, as most of us are tired
and ready for a night to merely avoid the German star shells
and lob an occasional barrage over to their side. Last night,
the Germans decided to focus on our sector and shelled us for
three solid hours. I spent much of the night in cover, wearing
my gas mask and dodging the bombs, but we did manage to
pitch a few shells and, I think, send a few Germans to their
unholy eternity. We are fighting like the coyote, desperate and
unrelenting and hopeful that soon, very soon, we will save
the world for democracy.

I am hesitant to address this next topic, but, as your future
husband, it is my duty to direct you toward righteousness.
My mother wrote me about a rather unpleasant altercation
in town where she mentioned you had placed yourself in
grave danger between two fighting men. Then she suggested,
and I pray in error, you may have ridden off with one of
them! I am grieved by these words, Lilly. I hope it is either
an erroneous report by my mother or a miscalculation in
judgment on your part. Whatever the case, I admonish you
to choose carefully your behavior. As my wife, you must set an
example for the community on proper and modest behavior
and not be fodder for gossip.

Of course, I know you are aware of this, and I trust you to
conduct yourself as the Christian lady I know you to be.

One other thing, Lilly. Mother mentioned your employ-
ment by the Torgesens as a dressmaker. Please, I beg of you, be
ready to cease this activity. It is not befitting a Christian
wife and mother to have an occupation. You will be busy
enough taking care of our children and home. I know perhaps

this is a hobby for now, while you wait for my return, and because of this, I will permit it. But when we are married, and I pray soon, you will have enough to occupy yourself—taking care of me!

I think of you always and commit you in good faith to our God in heaven to honor our plans and reunite us once again.

Love,
Reggie

sixteen

Perhaps it was exhaustion from the sun sucking every ounce of energy as she trudged toward the Torgesen T. Maybe it was fresh guilt, churned up at the reading of Reggie's letter. Or, it could have been the hope of seeing Heinrick. Lilly couldn't put her hands around the exact reason, but regardless, knots twisted her stomach by the time she reached the Torgesen ranch.

"I need a new dress!" Mrs. Torgesen exclaimed after she'd piled Lilly's lap full of new editions of *Ladies Home Journal* and *Butterick Fashions*.

Something *nouveau* and fabulous." Mrs. Torgesen's eyes twinkled as she wiggled her pudgy fingers at her. "Get to work."

Lilly flipped through the pages, determined to make Mrs. Torgesen look better than a willow tree this time around. Mrs. Torgesen headed for the kitchen.

After examining fashions from velvet empire skirts to long-neck prairie blouses with poet sleeves and French cuffs, she decided upon a two-piece suit, ankle length, with a double-breasted jacket. She showed it to Mrs. Torgesen, who drooled on the page, then Lilly buried herself in the fabric wardrobe for over an hour measuring scraps. She finally settled on brown and beige twill for the jacket and a skirt of brown wool.

She spent the rest of the morning piecing together a muslin pattern from scraps until she'd produced a pinned-together likeness of the skirt and jacket.

"When will I have my first fitting, Lilly?"

"Next week, perhaps. I think I can have the skirt ready to fit by then."

Mrs. Torgesen sat at the kitchen table, eating a fresh peach like an apple. Juice pooled at the corners of her mouth and dripped off her wrist. The humid kitchen absorbed the rich aroma and spiced the air. At the stove, Eleanor was steaming jars and parboiling a pot of peaches for canning. Stacked near the door were three wooden crates of fresh peaches, wrapped in green paper. Lilly couldn't help but to stare longingly at Mrs. Torgesen's peach. The Clark family would have no peach preserves this winter.

"Would you like a peach, Lilly?" Mrs. Torgesen gestured toward the crates.

Lilly shook her head. "Oh, no thank you, Mrs. Torgesen." She didn't know why, but suddenly she felt as if accepting the peach would be traitorous to the entire Clark family. She already felt like Benedict Arnold.

Mrs. Torgesen shrugged. Lilly gathered up the fabric and folded it into a canvas bag.

The noon sun burned the prairie until even the crickets hissed in protest. Lilly noticed a clump of Holstein on the horizon as she left the Torgesen T. She hadn't seen Heinrick, and an errant thought escaped, *Where is he?* Seeing Heinrick would only open the crusty scar upon her heart. Yet, she couldn't ignore the shard of disappointment that seemed to wedge deeper with each step away from the ranch.

A sharp whinny caught her ears. Lilly stiffened. She hadn't seen Clive at the Torgesen T either, but he was never far off. She quickened her pace, not looking back, but the thunder of hoofbeats beat down upon her. Lilly gritted her teeth and whirled, intending to meet the brute head on.

"You look angry, Lilly." Heinrick reined his mount, pushed up his hat, and leaned on his saddle horn.

Lilly gaped, then clamped her mouth closed. A thousand words rushed to mind, but not one could be formed upon her lips. Instead, Lilly balled her fists, fixed them onto her hips.

"You *are* mad." Heinrick's crooked white grin faded. "I'm sorry I didn't show up, I. . ." He glanced away, across the golden-brown prairie. "I just couldn't make it, that's all."

Lilly's bottled fury erupted. "I guess it didn't matter that I put my reputation, not to mention my future, on the line for you! You don't feel like it, so you don't show up? Do you think I'm bored and needed some cheering up? Or did you just determine to pester me with all that talk about God and my religion?" Lilly crossed her arms across her chest, squeezing hard to smother her anger. "Well, it just so happens, Mr. Zook, that I was planning on telling you that you know enough English and you can learn to read just fine on your own." Lilly turned on her heel, shaking. He would have to ride away now, and she wouldn't have to worry about him one day longer, him or his probing spiritual questions.

Her knees shook when she heard him dismount and felt his presence edge in on her, ushered in by the smell of soap and a tinge of masculine perspiration. He placed a hand on her shoulder and gently turned her around. She glued her eyes to his scuffed boots, refusing to betray what might be hidden in her eyes.

"I'm sorry, Lilly. I *am* grateful for all you did for me. Please forgive me."

Lilly squinted at him. He looked stricken.

His pitiful posture turned Lilly's heart. "Okay. I forgive you."

His crooked grin reappeared. "Thank you. Now, come riding with me."

"When, right now?"

Heinrick nodded "I have to ride fence this afternoon down near your place. Come with me."

Lilly's jaw dropped. "Are you sick, Heinrick? Have you heard one thing I've said to you? I can't be seen with you anymore. I'm going to marry another man!"

Heinrick raised his blond eyebrows and peered at her as if she was the one with the sickness. "I'm not courting you, Lilly. I just miss your company." His mouth flattened into a line. "But of course, I understand. I don't want to force you into anything; I just thought it might be, well, fun." Heinrick pulled on the brim of his hat. "It sure was good seeing you again, though."

Regret boiled in her chest as she watched him ride away.

She felt as if she'd been offered the priceless pearl, turned it down, and would never be the same for it. A compelling urge told her to call him back, to ride with him under the full view of the sun, and not be afraid.

"Heinrick!"

He reined his horse, turned, and smiled.

seventeen

Heinrick didn't allow Lilly time to change her mind. "Stay here, I'll be right back." With a whoop, he galloped back to the Torgesen T to saddle another mount. Lilly shrank into the shade of an aging ash and fought her swelling emotions. She kept telling herself he was just a friend, her student, and they were only taking a ride through the fields on a sunny day. But her stomach fluttered, and she couldn't deny the music in her heart.

Heinrick returned with a gray speckled mare tethered by her reins to his saddle horn.

"Do you know how to ride?"

"I've ridden Lucy a few times." She tied her bag to the mare's saddle.

Heinrick helped her place her foot in the stirrup, and she slid on, sidesaddle.

"We won't go fast."

It felt awkward and unsteady to be halfway on a horse, and Lilly struggled to find the rhythm. "I wish I was wearing my riding skirt," she muttered. Beside her, Heinrick erupted in honeyed laughter.

They meandered through Torgesen grazing land, which rolled like giant waves toward the Missouri riverbed.

"Someone once told me the Dakota prairie was like the ocean, endless and constantly moving," Lilly commented. The sun overhead winked at her. Prairie grass crunched under the horses' sturdy hooves, and a lonely meadowlark called to them, hidden in a clump of goldenrod. Lilly pushed her straw hat off her head, letting it dangle down her back by a long loop of ribbon. The wind fingered her braided hair. Beside her, Heinrick hummed softly.

"Perhaps," he finally agreed. "The prairie does seem to be constantly moving, and the wind is louder here than on the ocean, more fierce. It roars." Heinrick followed the movement of a circling hawk. "Look, Lilly," he said, "watch the hawk. Where it is, you will always find food."

Lilly's mouth went dry. "What did you say?"

Heinrick's voice was an ocean away. "My father and I used to hunt in Germany when I was young. He told me that, and I've never forgotten it."

Lilly nodded slowly, her heart thundering. The sun began to glare. The hot wind stung her face. "It's not a thing you forget, I suppose," she said weakly.

Heinrick continued, as if lost in a memory. "The hawk reminds me of the seagulls, soaring above the seascape. The sea seemed endless, like the prairie, but much more unforgiving. I was sick for fourteen days."

Heinrick reined his horse to a stop on a small bluff. Lilly took in an unmarred view of the Clark homestead and, farther on, the Pratt farm. Heinrick pointed to a "V" in the horizon. "That's the end of Torgesen land, and the little black line running along the hills is the railroad. See how it disappears behind that bluff?"

Shading her eyes, Lilly nodded. She hardened herself to the guilt that nipped at her, reborn by Heinrick's words—Reggie's words!—and focused on Heinrick's voice.

Heinrick now pointed past her own home. "The train reappears there and runs all the way into Mobridge." He shook his head. "I hear the railroad connects one end of the country to the other. Amazing."

Lilly wasn't examining the railroad tracks. She saw only Heinrick and his blue eyes. They were almost transparent, as if she could see inside him to his optimist's heart. He wore a faded bronze shirt, untied at the neck, and had pushed his brown bandana around so that the knot seemed a little bow tie at the base of his thick, tanned neck. He wore leather gloves, but his sleeves were rolled past the elbow to reveal muscled forearms. Weathered tan chaps covered his strong legs, and he seemed to be almost one with his mount. But Lilly was especially drawn in by his voice and an accent that betrayed a man who had surmounted fear, climbed aboard a ship, ridden over an angry sea, and was forging out a life in a hostile land.

"I want to work on the railroad someday, Lilly," he said softly. "I want to ride those black rails from shore to shore and see America. Discover why my relatives left Norway for America."

"Heinrick, why did you stand me up?"

Heinrick's gaze fell away from her, and a shadow crossed his face. "Clive needed the barn mucked out."

Lilly's heart twisted and shame eclipsed the anger she'd felt. "I'm sorry."

He lifted his gaze to hers, and she saw in his eyes a passionate blaze that betrayed his frustration. "Christmas, Lilly," he said. "By Christmas, I'll be free!" He suddenly whooped and spurred his horse, which shot off into a gallop along the ridgeline. Lilly clucked to her mare, and the horse cantered after him. She clutched the saddle horn and tried to swallow her terror.

"Move with her, Lilly. Don't be afraid." The wind brought his voice to her. "Give her some rein!"

"That's easy for you to say, you're not riding in a dress!"

Heinrick's laughter formed a vivid trail, one she could have followed with her eyes closed. He slowed his mount to a walk.

"Give your horse some freedom to move, Lilly. She wants to obey you, but if you choke her, she has no choice but to fight. Your horse has to be controlled by you, but you have to give her room to trust you. A horse that is afraid and choking on the bit is a horse that can't be ridden."

Lilly fingered the leather reins, loosening her hold. Her mare fell into a graceful walk next to Heinrick.

"It's like faith in God, Lilly. You are like that horse. You have to trust God, who loves you. No matter what He does, it is for your eternal good. You can't make God do what you want, just like your horse can't make you obey. The rider is the master of the horse, but the horse can make things a lot harder by grabbing the bit in her mouth and running off with it. A horse that won't surrender freely can't be used and is no good." Heinrick leaned over and put a hand on her reins. A crooked smile creased his face. "We shoot horses like that."

Lilly grimaced. Heinrick winked at her, his eyes twinkling in the sunlight. Then his smile vanished.

"You have to trust in God's love to fully surrender to His leading. Without that trust, you'll constantly be trying to grab the bit."

Lilly ran her eyes along the horizon. The fence line hurtled the next ridge and ran beyond that to the Clark farm. The joy had evaporated from the afternoon ride. First the reminder of Reggie and now Heinrick's spiritual invasion. Couldn't he just leave her religion alone? Why did he have to rattle her beliefs every time they were together?

"Lilly, do you trust that God loves you?"

Lilly shrugged and turned away. Tears edged her eyes.

"What's wrong?" His soft voice caressed her fraying emotions. His saddle creaked as he dismounted. He stood next to her, holding her reins, searching her eyes. Lilly bit her lip and turned her face away. Heinrick pulled off his glove and took her hand.

"Did I say something wrong?"

She shook her head but couldn't form words. How could she explain something she couldn't even understand herself? Of course, God loved her; the Bible said so, right? And Rev. Larsen had spelled it out so many times, she didn't have room for doubt. Believe and obey. She did both.

Then why did Heinrick's religion seem so different from hers? She was envious of Heinrick's absolute confidence of God's love. God's love to her had always meant tangible blessings, life in control. If Reggie died, did that mean God didn't love her? Lilly frowned at the turquoise, cloudless sky.

Why did Heinrick have to challenge everything? He'd

practically accused her of not being a Christian! He'd ripped apart her religion until it was shredded. Now she didn't know what she believed.

Two betraying tears sneaked down her cheeks. Heinrick wiped one away with his wide thumb. "What is it, Lilly?"

Lilly grabbed his wrist and pulled his hand away. She shook her head, until, abruptly, the fear shuddered out of her. "No, I don't know God loves me, and I'm afraid! I'm afraid I can't be everything He wants me to be, that I will somehow destroy my chance at happiness, maybe even my salvation! And I'm afraid He's going to let something bad happen, maybe even because of something I've done, and it'll ruin everything." The truth thinned her voice to sobs.

Heinrick's brows puckered. "Lilly, God does love you. He wants to give you salvation *and* a happy future. You just have to trust Him."

Lilly shook her head. "How do I trust Him if I don't know what He's going to do?"

"You trust Him because He's already shown you His love. And you can count on that."

Lilly frowned and bit her lip. How had God shown her His love? She dared to look at Heinrick. Compassion swam in his blue eyes, and, in that moment, all she wanted to do was slide off the mare and into his strong arms. And that frightened her almost as much as surrendering to an uncontrollable God.

"Heinrick, I have to go home. This is no good. I can't be here with you. I'm going to ruin everything."

Lilly leaned on his shoulders and slid off the horse. Then she stepped away. "Thank you for the ride."

"Lilly, you aren't going to cause Reggie to be killed by going for a ride with me."

Lilly's heart lodged in her chest. She stared at him, horrified. He'd summed up, in his statement, every nightmare she'd ever imagined.

"Do you think you can earn God's favor or His love by

following all the rules? By doing all Reggie, your parents, and your church tell you to?"

Heinrick pulled off his hat. The wind picked through his matted hair. "Your salvation is not based on anything you do, Lilly. No one can be good enough to be saved. That's why Jesus came and allowed Himself to be crucified. No one can live up to the Jewish law. It only serves to point out our sins. But Jesus sets us free from death by paying the price for our sins. All we can do is ask for forgiveness and receive salvation! We cannot earn it. Salvation isn't a bargain with God, it's a gift from Him."

Lilly saw him through watery eyes.

Heinrick wrapped his massive hands around her upper arms. "I don't know much, Lilly, but I know this. It is by grace you are saved through faith. Grace, Lilly. Something unearned, undeserved, and without rules." His voice was like the wind, refreshing and tugging at the bonds of her soul. "If you truly want to follow God and to know Him, then you have to understand this. If there is nothing we can do to earn salvation, if Jesus paid for our sins before we knew Him, when we were the *worst* of sinners, then there is also nothing we can do to lose it. His sacrifice is enough to pay for *all* of our sins. You cannot ruin your salvation because it is not in your power to ruin it! He loves you, and there is nothing you can do about it."

Lilly gasped as the truth hit her heart. She felt the first inklings of a freedom she'd been searching for all her life. "Not in my power to ruin it?"

Heinrick lifted her chin with his forefinger, and his gaze held hers. "God loves you, Lilly. You can trust His plans; for you, for Reggie, for your life."

She nodded, then slipped under his arms and started toward home. Halfway across the Clark hayfield, she began to laugh, joy bubbling from some broken vault in her soul. Lilly opened her arms, embracing the sky, twirled twice, and broke into a run. The canvas bag bumped against her back as she went leaping across the fallow field, laughing, crying, and most of all singing, as her soul, for the first time, found freedom.

That night, after Bonnie's breath deepened in sleep beside her, Lilly slipped out of her bed and onto her knees. Embedded in the glow of moonlight, Lilly prayed and, for the first time in her life, fully surrendered to the One who loved her.

eighteen

The melody of an early rising bluebird floated in on a cool dawn breeze. Lilly awakened slowly, bathed in the peace of a new morning, and realized she'd slept straight through. No nightmare. The terrifying dream had vanished, as had the fear that seemed to dog her since Reggie's departure. Worry still throbbed on one side of her heart, but it wasn't the same frantic panic that had boiled in her soul.

The second thing that impressed her as she sat up and gazed at her light-dappled walls, was the unfamiliar, remarkable lightness of soul, as if the day was hers and nothing could pin her down. It was the intoxicating breath of unconditional love, giving her hope wings. It made her gasp.

Bonnie sat up next to her, rubbing her eyes. "What?"

Lilly whirled and embraced her sister. They fell together on the stuffed mattress and giggled.

Lilly threw off the sheet, skipped to the window, and pulled back the curtains. The shadow of the house loomed long across the yard, but the sun lit the field rose gold. "With each sunrise, there is new hope."

Bonnie stared at her as if she'd grown another leg.

Lilly pulled off her cotton nightgown. She needed something refreshing, something sunny. She chose a one-piece cornflower blue calico with minute yellow daisies. It had a fitted bodice, with a lace-trimmed boat neck and turned-up cap sleeves. Lilly slid it over her head, then loosely braided her hair down her back.

"You going somewhere?" Bonnie asked, her knees drawn up to her chest under the sheet.

"Going out to greet the dawn."

Lilly reckoned, from Bonnie's look, she must have turned

purple. But she didn't care. On impulse, she grabbed her Bible and tucked it under her arm. Then she left her bewildered sister to flop back onto the feather pillow and tiptoed down the stairs.

Lilly's mother was in the kitchen whipping pancake batter. She glanced up, spied Lilly, and her brow knit into a frown. Lilly shot her a wide smile and stepped out onto the porch. Across the yard, the barn doors were open, her father inside, milking. Lilly headed toward her maple grove.

The wind whispered in the branches, and the glade was cool and shadowed. Lilly strolled to the bluff and stared out at the endless prairie. A hazy residue of platinum, rose, and lavender simmered along the eastern horizon. From the opposing shore, a startled pheasant took flight from a clump of sage. Hope rode the air, tinged in the fragrance of columbine and jasmine, which continued to bloom in hardy defiance of the drought.

Lilly sat on a piece of driftwood to read her Bible. She had no idea what she was doing, but it seemed the right thing to do. Like Heinrick said, if she was to trust God, she ought to know Him. And Heinrick seemed to think knowing God meant more than just attending services. She randomly flipped open the thick Bible and determined to give it a try.

She landed somewhere in the Old Testament. Jeremiah. She hardly recalled the book, but ran her finger down the page. Then, to her profound surprise, she noticed someone had marked a verse. Verse eleven of chapter twenty-nine was underlined ever so slightly in pencil, and she heard her heart thump as she read. "For I know the thoughts that I think toward you, saith the LORD, thoughts of peace, and not of evil, to give you an expected end. Then shall ye call upon me, and ye shall go and pray unto me, and I will hearken unto you. And ye shall seek me, and find me, when ye shall search for me with all your heart."

A shiver rippled up Lilly's spine. *"Ye shall seek me, and find me, when ye shall search for me with all your heart."* Lilly bit her lip and looked up at the pale, jeweled sky. Could the Maker of the heavens really be talking to her, calling out to her? "The Living Word," Heinrick had said. God talking through the Bible. The thought was terrifying and exhilarating and beyond her comprehension.

Lilly bowed her head. *Yes, God. I want to seek You. I want to find You. I know You love me, and I want to surrender to You and Your plans for me.*

As she lifted her eyes, the fragrance of peace swept through her heart. She drew in a long breath, and the feeling seeped into her bones. But would it linger when the heat of day battered it, when fear reared its head in the form of news from Europe? Would she be able to trust?

This surrender would have to be a daily, moment-by-moment thing. *God, please, help me to know You so I am not afraid, so I see Your love. Help me to trust You.*

It was the briefest of moments after the prayer left her lips that she realized she must tell Reggie. Everything. The half-truths of her letters were, simply put, sin. She had to be honest. Most of all, she had to share with him the joy of grace. Maybe it would give him the one thing he so desperately needed—release from the cold knot of fear.

She would write to him on lavender paper, send a pressed lily, and hope he would truly understand her newfound joy.

Most of all, she would pray somehow the news of her spiritual awakening would cushion the tale about Heinrick. To tell Reggie the truth, she would have to tell him about her German friend. She would put her surrender, that peace, to the test and trust the Lord for the outcome.

Lilly stood, flung out her arms as if to welcome the day, and then picked her way through the grove of maples and back to the Clark farm for breakfast.

❧

Lilly spent the morning laying out and cutting the skirt for Mrs. Torgesen's suit on the kitchen table. Lilly's mother peeked over her shoulder, offered a few hints, and finally admitted to Lilly that she'd surpassed her mother as a seamstress.

"I don't know how you can just look at a picture and make it come alive." Her mother shook her head in parental admiration.

After a lunch of warm milk, bread, and jam, Lilly escaped to her room and wrote to Reggie. The story was more difficult in the telling than she'd anticipated, and it took her two full hours to fill two evenly scrawled pages. She started over twice and finally resigned herself to the reality that regardless how she wrote it, she'd betrayed him. She'd spent a week in the company of a man not her fiancé, despite its innocence, and she would have to hope Reggie trusted her. She slipped a sprig of lily of the valley into the envelope. Its tiny white bells were withering, but the fragrance lingered. She hoped Reggie would be encouraged by it. She sealed the letter and propped it on her vanity. She couldn't mail it until Monday's train, but she felt that much the cleaner for having revealed the truth.

"Lilly, could you run into Ernestine's for flour and molasses?" her mother called from the bottom steps. Lilly grabbed her basket and her straw hat and set off for Mobridge.

A buzz of tension, beyond the hum of the riverbed grasshoppers, drifted through the town. Horses were packed into tight rows, tethered to hitching posts. Buckboards stood at a standstill, filled with goods. Women in bonnets and men chewing on straw milled about on the clapboard sidewalk. Curious, Lilly quickened her pace toward Ernestine's.

The news met her there.

"Did you hear about the battle?" Ernestine's fat sweaty hands worked quickly, filling the flour sacks. Lilly handed her the empty burlap bag she'd borrowed. Ernestine took it and continued her monologue. "We just got the news in the *Milwaukee Journal*. A big battle over a river in France someplace." She gave Lilly the flour. Her probing eyes seemed to soften. "They say our boys are in the fray."

Lilly bit her lip and nodded. "Can I have some molasses, also?"

Ernestine turned and searched the shelves for a bottle. Lilly was glad for the moment to compose herself. Her heartbeat throbbed in her ears, and she fought a tremble. Ernestine returned with the molasses. Lilly dropped it into her basket and paid her.

"God be with you and Reggie." Ernestine offered a smile that felt too much like a condolence.

"Thank you," Lilly managed. She darted for the door.

At Miller's, Ed shrugged. "Sorry, Lilly, we're out of fresh newspapers. Try the postal."

Lilly hustled to the post office and discovered they, too, were sold out. Heart sinking, she headed for the door.

"Lilly, you have a letter." Mildred Baxter, the postmistress, handed her a small envelope.

Lilly frowned. "Did I miss the train?"

Mildred shook her head. "I don't know who it's from."

Lilly stepped out into the sunshine, confusion distracting her disappointment over the shortage of newspapers. The letter *was* for her. Her name was spelled out in small, bold capitals on the bleached parchment envelope. And there was no postage.

Lilly examined it for a moment, then decided to open it on the road home, away from any prying eyes on the street. She slipped the letter into her basket.

Her last stop was the armory. She found Marjorie red-eyed and folding bandages with unequalled passion. Lilly pulled her friend into an embrace.

"Don't worry, Marj. God will watch over them."

Tears flooded Marjorie's eyes. "That doesn't mean Harley will come back home. It doesn't mean everything will be okay."

Lilly peered into her friend's anguished face, her heart reciting everything she'd embraced over the past day. "Yes, it does. God loves us, and because of that, everything will be okay."

Marjorie studied her a long moment, as if absorbing her words. Then she laid her head on Lilly's shoulder. Lilly held her, briefly bearing her friend's burden. Then Lilly left Marjorie to assemble soon-to-be needed action kits and headed home.

⁂

A half-mile out of Mobridge, Lilly remembered the letter. She retrieved it from the basket and worked the envelope open.

It was from Heinrick.

Dear Lilly,
*   I never thanked you for the lessons. Please meet me at our "school" tomorrow night at sunset.*

                                        Your friend,
                                        Heinrick

Lilly's mouth dried, and she nearly allowed the wind to snatch the letter from her grip. In some strange, awkward way, his invitation was a soothing balm on the worry tearing at her heart; as if time with Heinrick could actually help her believe the words she'd so confidently spoken to Marjorie— that God would make everything okay.

She ambled home, attempting to unsnarl the paradox in her heart.

nineteen

With the news of the ongoing battle in France, worry moved into the Clark home. It brought with it a foul mood. Olive did nothing but clutch Christian and sit on the porch in the wide willow rocker, staring with glassy eyes out over the dead wheat field. Her father and Frankie rose long before dawn to cut prairie grass. Her mother canned three dozen jars of gooseberry jam, her lips moving in constant prayer. Lilly basted together, in wide stitches, Erica Torgesen's skirt and hoped she would have a happy occasion to wear it to, instead of a funeral.

Lilly had greeted the dawn by the river, praying and watching the sun creep over the horizon from Reggie's side of the world. Her morning reading, from Psalm 56, seemed a shield against the barrage of the day. "What time I am afraid, I will trust in thee. In God I will praise his word, in God I have put my trust; I will not fear what flesh can do unto me." God certainly knew how to meet the need of the moment. Lilly memorized the verse and recited it often, especially when worry curled around her heart like a stinging nettle.

The day drew out like old honey. Although anxiety strummed in her heart, Lilly couldn't deny that time crawled in response to the anticipation of seeing Heinrick. Curiosity ran like wildfire through her thoughts. More than that, however, she longed for his calming presence to remind her of God's love. Somehow, Heinrick could see into her soul, unearth her deepest fears, and scatter them with a word of wisdom.

Dinner was sober and simple: new potatoes, hot bread, and gravy. Lilly made a salad from carrots and dandelion greens. Olive excused herself to her room, and Bonnie cleared the table. Lilly washed the dishes in silence, but her heart thundered with the ticks of the mantle clock. Finally, the last dish sparkled, and she dashed upstairs. She changed into a jade green skirt and white blouse with a Buster Brown collar and puffy short sleeves.

Lilly noticed her mother glance up from her knitting and raise her thin brows as Lilly flew past her on the porch.

Heinrick was waiting, embedded in the shadows of a great maple. He'd spiffed up for the occasion, a pair of clean black trousers, polished boots, a brown cotton button-down shirt, albeit frayed at the elbows, and a fringed dark chocolate leather vest. He'd even slicked back his golden hair. He gave her a wide grin and stepped from the arms of the tree.

"*Guten Abend*, Lilly." His voice was warm, and he offered her his arm.

"Hello, Heinrick," Lilly returned, suddenly gripped with shyness. She lowered her eyes, but wrapped her arm around the crook of his elbow. He led her out onto the bluff, then down to their cottonwood bench. The sun melted along the horizon, and the air smelled faintly of drying hay.

He didn't look at her, but instead chose a family of prairie dogs, darting along the other shore, for his attention. "I wanted to thank you, Lilly," he started in a halting voice. "You've given me my future. If I can read, I can do anything. I know it cost you to meet me, and I will never forget your sacrifice."

Lilly considered him, her gaze running along his wide-set jaw and his blond hair curling behind his ears. His shirt-sleeves tightened around the base of his muscled arms, and he had his hands folded in his lap. She remembered the way those hands had caught the blows of the Craffey brothers, tamed a wild stallion, batted away Clive's anger, and tenderly wiped a tear from her cheek. So powerful, yet profoundly gentle. She may have taught him how to read, but he'd taught her how to live.

"I have to thank you, also." Lilly gazed toward the melting sunset. "I did it, Heinrick. I prayed and surrendered to God's love." She glanced at him. His eyes drew her in and held her. They were filled with a vivid, tangible joy, and in that moment, she saw herself as he saw her. Not as Reggie's fiancée, or as a farm girl, or even as his teacher, but as a lady he admired. She knew, as long as she lived, she would never forget the way Heinrick made her believe she was special. . .and loved. Then he smiled, and she could have danced in the music of it. Heinrick reached into his vest pocket. "I have a gift for you." He pulled out a wad of cotton and held it out to her.

Lilly unwrapped it carefully and gasped. Inside lay a long-toothed, hand-painted, brass butterfly comb, with an emerald-colored glass stone in the center. Wide wings, painted a ginger brown, flared from the center stone body. At the bottom, a brass tail was fashioned into a row of delicate loops. It was antique, exquisite, and doubtlessly expensive.

"It's breathtaking," Lilly whispered.

"It belonged to my mother."

Lilly's eyes teared. "I don't know what to say. I can't accept it."

Heinrick frowned. "Why not?"

Lilly bit her lip. Why not? It was just a gift from a friend, a sort of payment for her kind deed. She felt herself shrugging. "I. . .I don't know."

"Please take it, Lilly. I want you to have it."

With trembling hands, she folded the comb carefully back into the cotton. "Thank you. I'll treasure it."

Heinrick smiled, and delight in his blue eyes. "Now, tell me about the dress you are making Erica Torgesen that has her waltzing around the ranch."

Lilly laughed, and together they sat on the cottonwood bench, knees touching, while she told him about Mrs. Torgesen, the willow tree dress, and her fashion dreams. Heinrick laughed and listened, resting his head on his hands as he watched her.

Twilight hued the Missouri copper. Lilly heard a voice threading through the maple grove, calling her name. A voice edged in panic.

Lilly jumped to her feet. "Over here, Bonnie." She cast a frown at Heinrick. "I have to go."

He nodded and scrambled up the bluff, then reached down for Lilly. Lilly climbed over the ridge just as Bonnie burst from the shadows. She skidded to a halt and stared at the pair, eyes bulging, mouth agape. She found her senses quickly, however, and turned her attention to Lilly. Her eyes were troubled and her voice shook. "Come home, Lilly."

"Bonnie, you're scaring me." Lilly wound her arms around herself.

Bonnie's eyes flooded and her chin quivered, but she managed an explanation. "Olive got a telegram. Chuck's been killed."

Lilly covered her mouth with her hand, stifling a cry of anguish. She felt Heinrick's arm wind around her waist.

"Lilly, that's not all." Bonnie paused and took a step toward Lilly, a hand extended as if to steady the news. "Rev. and Mrs. Larsen are up at the house."

The blood drained from Lilly's face.

"Reggie's missing."

twenty

Lilly leaned back on her heels and rubbed a grimy wrist across her sweaty brow. Her body felt dry and dusty, and her hands were cracked and sore from pulling weeds. But the sting in her palms felt easier to bear than the searing wounds in her heart. Each member of her family dodged the specter of grief in their own way. While Lilly tediously weeded the dying garden, her father worked from dawn 'til dusk in the hay field, dragging an exhausted Frankie with him. Her mother canned thirty-six jars of dills and twelve of relish, DJ chased the kittens around the dry yellowing yard and played with Christian, and Olive stopped living. She was a wasteland, crushed in spirit and hope, withering by the hour. She ceased eating and, after the first day, stopped dressing. By Sunday, she wouldn't even rise from her double bed. Lilly brought her meals, stroked her sister's waist-long chestnut hair, and tried to comfort her. But for Olive, there was no solace. To Lilly, she was a frightening prophecy of what might come if Reggie was confirmed dead. Lilly clung to the hope, should that dark hour transpire, her newfound peace would carry her above the grave and keep her from being, in essence, Olive, a woman who believed she had no tomorrows.

Lilly buried herself in the Psalms. It seemed a desperate escape at first, and Lilly doubted that the Bible would offer her any sort of encouragement. She was infinitely mistaken. The never-before-read passages became nearly tangible in their spiritual embrace and, as she wound herself inside the sorrows and joys of the Jewish king, David, she reaped the one thing Olive lacked—faith. David praised God in the midst of sorrow, and she would as well, clutching the belief that God loved her.

&

"It's addressed to Lillian Clark." Bonnie's face was ashen as she handed Lilly the telegram. Lilly took the envelope with shaking hands. Two weeks without a word and finally the army had sent news. It must have taken them that long to sift through the bodies.

Her mother crept up beside Lilly and wound an arm around her waist. "Open it, Honey."

As the last embers of hope died within her, Lilly worked the telegram open. Brutally short, it was from the person she least expected to hear from.

Dear Lilly,
   Alive. In Paris hospital. Harley KIA. Chuck KIA. Coming home.

Reggie

Lilly gasped, covered her mouth, and sank into a kitchen chair. She handed the telegram to her mother, who read it aloud and wept.

Hot tears ran down Lilly's cheeks. God had saved Reggie. He was coming home. She wrapped her arms around herself and pushed back a tremble.

"Oh, Lilly! It's so wonderful!" Bonnie squealed and embraced her, and Lilly's father squeezed Lilly's shoulder as he passed by. Only Olive was speechless. She stood at the end of the table, looking brutal in her bathrobe and wadded, greasy hair. Lilly glanced at her and, in that instant, felt her sister's jealousy as if it were a right-handed blow.

Lilly offered a sympathetic smile, but Olive's disbelieving eyes tightened into a glare. She whirled and ran to her room.

The only thing left to do was to tell Marjorie. Dread weighted Lilly's footsteps all the way to the Pratt farm. When she rapped on the peeling screen door, Mrs. Pratt opened it and greeted her cheerfully. When she saw Lilly's face, however, she ushered her to the kitchen, then sent

Evelyn into town to fetch Marjorie.

Why it had been ordained for Lilly to inform her best friend her fiancé had been killed, she would never understand. It seemed utterly unfair to be shouldered with the job. And yet, she knew the hope she'd just discovered and so desperately clung to was the only hope she could offer her friend. She longed to tell Marjorie that God could not only comfort her, He could create a future for her despite the destruction of her well-laid plans.

Marjorie read the telegram twice and handed it back to Lilly. Her hands shook. "Maybe he's mistaken."

"Maybe." But doubt filled Lilly's reply. Marjorie heard it, and her mourning wail shredded Lilly's heart. Marjorie crumpled into Lilly's arms and sobs shuddered through her. Lilly rubbed her hair and mourned with her as the horror of war shattered their hearts.

Lilly finally tucked a spent Marjorie into bed. Wandering home under a starlit sky, she listened to the breeze moan in her ears and wondered what tomorrow would bring.

Chuck and Harley were gone, but Reggie was coming home. It was a sign. God wanted them together. She would obey, even though she only saw Heinrick each night in her dreams.

&

Alice Larsen visited a few days later, recovered from her grief and unfurling dramatic plans for Lilly's wedding. She was aghast to discover Lilly hadn't started on her wedding dress.

"I would think, with your love of sewing, you would have it cut out and basted, at least."

Lilly smiled and mentioned she was helping Erica Torgesen with a dress. Mrs. Larsen waved the thought away with the back of her hand. "You'll just have to tell Erica Torgesen you are much too busy now to dress her up like a doll. She's too concerned with frills, anyway." Mrs. Larsen laid a hand on Mrs. Clark's arm and, looking at Lilly, breathed into her mother's corner of the table, "It's as if she thinks life is a fashion show!"

Lilly and her mother exchanged looks and smiled. That was exactly what Erica Torgesen thought.

"Even so, Mrs. Larsen, I promised her an outfit, and I intend to finish it," Lilly said.

Mrs. Larsen recoiled as if Lilly had slapped her. "Well, I know you like to sew, Lilly, but really, your priorities are with Reggie, now that he is coming home. I thought he'd written to you as much."

Lilly gaped. Was Reggie duplicating his letters to her to his mother? She quickly clamped her mouth shut and folded her hands on the table. "Reggie and I will discuss it when he returns."

Mrs. Larsen gave her a disapproving look. "You shouldn't have to *discuss* anything with Reggie. He's your husband, and your job is to obey."

"He's not my husband yet, Mrs. Larsen."

Mrs. Larsen gasped, but recovered in lightning speed. "And he may not be with that attitude!" She shot a glance at Lilly's mother, who'd planted a smile on her face.

"Well." Mrs. Larsen pounced to her feet. She seemed to search for words. "Good day, then."

Lilly stood. "Good day, Mrs. Larsen." She smiled, but Mrs. Larsen did not.

"I hope to see some progress on that dress and the wedding plans when I return."

Lilly nodded as if that was exactly what Mrs. Larsen could expect. The woman let the screen door bang behind her.

Mother Clark's smile faded as she eyed her daughter. "Is there something you want to tell me?"

"Of course not, Mother," Lilly replied in a thin voice.

❧

She was just confused. Things were happening too fast—Reggie's telegram, Chuck's death, the elaborate Alice Larsen–created wedding plans. Lilly lay on her bed, staring at the ceiling. Confusion was the only reasonable explanation for the heaviness that settled over her when she thought about life with Reggie. She was just feeling rushed, all her dreams cascading upon her. Even her prayers seemed to be hitting the ceiling and bouncing back.

She determined to count her blessings and make Reggie's homecoming everything he and Mrs. Larsen hoped it would be.

August slid by without a word from Reggie, or Heinrick, for that matter. The cessation of Reggie's letters lit worry in Lilly's heart. She wondered if perhaps Reggie had been mistaken about his homeward destination. September rode in, carrying with it the crisp, expectant fall air. Lilly finished Erica Torgesen's suit, but turned her down when Mrs. Torgesen asked for a Thanksgiving outfit.

Mrs. Torgesen frowned her disappointment. "Why, Dear?"

Lilly forced a smile. "Because I plan to be getting married right about then."

A delighted Mrs. Torgesen clasped both hands to her mouth, then embraced Lilly.

Lilly tarried as she left the Torgesen T the final time. She leaned on the corral and watched Buttercup run among the group of stock horses, obviously the master of the herd. The mustang trotted near, stopping five feet away to examine her. His glassy brown eyes seemed to search hers, and she extended a hand to him. He sputtered and backed away.

Lilly withdrew her hand. Well, she understood. Her heart seemed just as skittish, afraid to step forward and be caught.

And yet, that was what she'd been waiting for her entire life.

She dragged home. The prairie grass had turned golden. The leaves were tarnished, the maples blushing red and orange. The smell of wood fires spiced the air. A skein of Canadian geese overhead honked their way south. Winter would soon shroud the prairie, with its endless whiteness and wind that seemed to scream in one eternal blast. Winter was for family, and quiet times, and embracing all hibernation had to offer. By then, she hoped, Reggie would be home, they would be married, and she would finally again know the sweet fragrance of peace.

twenty-one

"May I walk home alone?" Lilly gathered her shawl over her shoulders and glanced up at her mother, who was tucking DJ into his woolen coat. Her mother met her gaze, compassion written on her face. She nodded.

Lilly let a sigh of relief escape her lips. The cool starlit night would be a refreshing change to Rev. Larsen's heated sermon.

The reverend's territory-wide announcement for all members of the congregation to meet and pray for the safety of their soldiers was a gathering meant to heal and extend hope to the hurting. The entire community, tired of harvesting a dying crop and weary of leaning on faith, mustered to the call, and the little church nearly burst to overflowing, yearning for fresh hope. Rev. Larsen, recognizing an opportune moment, preached a pointed sermon about obedience. It seemed to Lilly every word was meant for her ears.

Over the past month, Alice Larsen had been dutiful in her visits, inspecting Lilly's progress on her wedding dress, as if Lilly was sewing together the older woman's hopes and dreams.

Lilly exited the church cloakroom. The cool autumn breeze nipped at her ears as she watched Dakotans scatter in all directions, walking or riding buckboards. Her parents, Frankie, DJ, and Bonnie in tow, hustled past her.

"Don't tarry too long," her mother whispered.

Main Street was lonely and deeply shadowed. As she meandered down the dirt street, early stars winked at her. Dying leaves hissed, stirred by the breeze. Lilly stared into the night sky, and emptiness panged in her heart. Despite her prayers and growing faith in God's love, her spirit seemed to be dying within her, and she'd never felt so despondent. "God, what's wrong with me? Why do I feel as though I am walking through a tunnel that's only getting darker? Why am I not rejoicing? Reggie is coming home. This is a gift from You!" She wrapped her arms around her waist and moaned. The sound was snagged by the wind and amplified. "Help me, Lord." The words seemed a catharsis, and, with them, she realized she needed God more than she ever had before. She needed Him to remind her He had it all worked out, that He was still in charge—that marrying Reggie was right and His ordained will. "Please, God, give me peace in my heart." Her words ended in muffled sobs as she buried her face in her hands.

"Lilly?"

Heinrick approached her dressed in a muddy ankle-length duster, and holding the reins to his stomping bay. He smiled, but his eyes betrayed worry.

"Where have you been?" She clamped a hand over her mouth, ashamed at the desperation in her voice.

"Roundup."

Lilly felt like a fool. All this time she thought he'd been ignoring her, hiding somewhere in a clump of Holsteins.

"I'm sorry, Heinrick. I just, well, missed you." There, she'd said it. And it was the truth. She could have used his kind words, his wisdom, and his nudges to trust in the Lord.

Heinrick looked stricken. He grabbed her by the arm. "I need to talk to you." Flinging his reins over a hitching post, he led her to the alley between Graham's Pharmacy and the armory. Lilly frowned as he stepped into the shadows, but followed. Camouflaged in the semidarkness, Heinrick blew out a heavy breath, turning her to face him. His hat was pushed back on his head, and his hair was an inch longer, caught in the collar of his coat. Thick, white-blond stubble layered his cheeks, and something disturbing darkened his eyes.

"Lilly, I'm sorry. I didn't tell you the whole truth."

Her brow knotted in confusion.

"I saw you when you came out to the Torgesen T the last time. But. . .well, I didn't want to see you, so I rode out, away from you."

Lilly's frown deepened, and she crossed her arms under her wool cape.

"I didn't want to hurt you, Lilly, or confuse us."

Us? "What are you talking about, Heinrick?"

He swept off his hat, rubbed the brim with his hands, and stared at the ground.

"I'm talking about you belonging to another man, Lilly. I'm talking about the fact you are pledged to marry someone else, and. . .I'm in love with you."

Her jaw dropped and a tremor rippled up her spine.

"But I can't have you." Heinrick's voice was hoarse, and he avoided her eyes. "And every time I see you, it feels like a knife turning in my chest."

Shock rocked Lilly to her toes. Then, like a fragrant breeze, the joy swept through her heart. Heinrick *loved* her. That was why his eyes twinkled with delight when she was with him, why his voice always turned tender, and why he now looked more afraid than she'd ever seen him, even when facing the Craffey brothers. And she knew why her own heart now felt suddenly, wonderfully, alive.

"Oh, Heinrick," Lilly blurted, unable to stop herself. "I love you, too."

Heinrick's blue eyes probed hers, searching for the truth.

Lilly smiled broadly, love coursing through her veins with every beat of her heart. "Ya, Heinrick, I do!"

His eyes shone as a lopsided grin appeared on his face. He closed the gap between them in one smooth step. Then he slid a gloved hand around her neck. She jumped, then leaned into his strong grip.

Heinrick studied her for a moment, as if imprinting her face on his memory, examining her eyes, her hair, her nose, finally her lips. The expression in his eyes betrayed his intentions.

He wanted to kiss her.

Lilly's breath caught in her throat and she tingled from head to toe. She felt frightened and hopeful all at once. She wanted to be inside his powerful arms, to feel the tenderness of his touch. But it was wrong. Despite her feelings and his, so vividly written on his face, she couldn't allow him to kiss her. Lilly touched his chest, intending to push him away.

"Lillian Clark, what are you doing?"

The voice ripped them apart. Heinrick stepped away from her as Lilly whirled. Marjorie Pratt stood on the street, next to the armory, staring at them as if they had planted a bomb on Main Street. "What are you doing?" she repeated, her voice rising in horror.

Lilly felt sick. "Marjorie, please."

"You are engaged to Reggie! And this man," Marjorie pointed wildly at Heinrick, "is a *German!* His kind *murdered* Harley and *Chuck* and almost killed Reggie, and you are *kissing* him?" Her voice reached a shrill pitch, and Lilly stepped toward her.

"Marjorie, I'm not kissing him. We're just talking."

"That's not what it looked like to me!"

Lilly shook her head, "Marj, please listen. . . ."

"I will *not* listen, you. . .you. . .*traitor!*" Marjorie glared at her, shaking with fury. Lilly saw Marjorie's rage and realized her friend was beyond reason. Then Marjorie bolted, plunging into the darkness. Lilly started after her, groaned, and let her go.

She turned and shot a helpless look at Heinrick. His defeated expression terrified her more than Marjorie's fury. Heinrick replaced his hat, his mouth set in a muted line. His eyes were distant. "I'll take you home."

Lilly wanted to scream, weep, throw herself into his arms, and make him affirm his love for her. But his emotions were locked safely behind the same tortured, lonely expression she'd seen back at the Torgesen T. This time, however, instead of reaching out to her, pulling her into his world, he pushed her away. Her eyes filled.

Heinrick helped her into the saddle, then mounted his horse behind her. His arms wrapped around her, and she let herself enjoy the strong, safe place inside his forced embrace. He said nothing the entire ride home, but Lilly felt his chest move in heavy sighs as she leaned against him. When she glanced up into his shadowed face, hoping to find a glimmer of the love he'd unveiled in the alley, she saw only stone blue eyes peering into the darkness.

The wind moaned, along with her heart. The smell of wood fires lingered in the air, and perhaps the smoke singed her eyes, for tears edged down her cheeks.

When they reached her road, Heinrick reined the bay. "Should I take you to the house?" His voice seemed pinched, as if pushed through a vice.

Lilly's throat burned. "No. I'd better get off here."

Heinrick nodded and dismounted. Lilly let herself slide into his arms. He held her one moment longer than necessary, or maybe she imagined it. Then he released her, and she stepped away. She lifted her chin, waiting for him to remount his horse. A thousand words formed, but she couldn't get them past the sorrow flooding her heart.

Heinrick grabbed his saddle horn and stared out across the prairie. "You were right, Lilly. I should have listened to you from the beginning. I seem to bring you nothing but trouble. I'm sorry."

Lilly longed to refute his words. *Oh no, Heinrick, you've brought me nothing but joy.* But she saw in his eyes the futility of argument.

"I think, for your sake," Heinrick's voice turned stiff, "and for mine, this is good-bye."

Lilly bit her lip and nodded woodenly.

"Lilly, don't forget God loves you." He kept the rest unspoken, but oh, how she wanted to hear it: *and so do I.*

She shivered as she watched him climb into the saddle. He spurred his horse and, in violent abruptness, was gone in a full gallop toward the Torgesen T.

Then there was just the terrible roaring of emptiness in her heart.

❧

By Lilly's estimation, the shelling started shortly after midnight.

The first rock shattered one of the glass windows on the front of the house and landed in the living room, next to her mother's willow rocker. The second volley destroyed the other window and smashed a stack of fine china her mother had carted west from Chicago.

By the time the third rock hurtled through the parlor window and crushed the mantle clock, her father was in the living room, pulling on his cotton workpants and flipping suspenders over his shoulders. Lilly watched from the doorway of her bedroom as her mother flew down the stairs, despite orders to stay put. Lilly realized her mother's intentions were not to save her collection of gel teacups from the old country nor the freshly caned straight-back chairs. No, she headed straight for Olive and Christian's room, located in the lean-to on the main floor.

Olive appeared, clutching a screaming Christian, her face the color of chalk. "What's going on?" she shrieked.

Mother Clark slung her arm around them. "Upstairs!" she commanded.

From the landing, Lilly clutched Bonnie's hand and watched them race for the stairway. A rock blew through the kitchen window, scattering glass at their heels. Olive's terrified scream shook the house.

"Hurry!" Lilly yelled.

Olive and her mother scampered up the stairs two at a time. Her older sister dove past Lilly and flew into her parents' room. Lilly saw her throw Christian on the bed and cover him with her body. Mrs. Clark grabbed Bonnie by the arm, meaning to pull both her girls along with her, but Lilly broke away from Bonnie's grasp and scrambled down the stairs.

"Lilly, come back here!" her mother called, racing down the hall to retrieve the boys.

Lilly skidded to a halt in the parlor. Her father was crouched below a window. He shot her a frown. "Get down."

She dropped to all fours and crawled across the floor. "Who's doing this?"

He put a finger to his lips.

Outside, Lilly heard slurred, enraged voices.

"That's Clive Torgesen!" Her chest tightened. A rock ripped through an unbroken pane and glass sprayed the room. Lilly cried out as her father shielded her with his body. The rock thudded into a Queen Anne armchair.

"I'm going out there," he said.

Lilly grabbed his arm. "No, Father, they'll kill you!"

He jerked his arm away. "I've got to stop them before they do real damage, like set fire to the house."

Lilly's heart froze in her chest.

Jumping up, she scuttled behind her father.

"Lilly, get upstairs!" He opened the front door.

She backed away and hid behind the parlor doorframe.

Her father stepped onto the porch. Lilly tiptoed to the front door, sidled to one side, and peeked out. In the moonlight, she could make out four men: Clive Torgesen, two of his cattle hands, and an older man. Lilly gasped. The last was Harry Bishop, Marjorie's cousin, and from latest accounts, an outlaw. Marjorie had obviously raced straight home and informed her family what she'd seen in Mobridge.

Mr. Clark held up a steady hand and spoke in a loud voice. "Howdy, boys. What seems to be the problem?"

Guilt edged Lilly onto the porch. This was her doing, and she had to face it.

Clive balled his hands on his hips and swayed. "Your daughter's a Benedict Arnold, Clark!"

"I have three daughters, boys, and all of them are loyal to the Red, White, and Blue." Her father's calm voice mustered Lilly's courage.

Harry pointed a quivering finger at him. "That ain't true! Marjorie caught her kissing a German right here in this very town!"

Lilly's breath caught, but she propelled her legs forward and darted behind her father, clutching his arm. The wind whipped through her cotton nightgown and even from five feet away, the pungent odor of whiskey hit her with a stinging force. Lilly's eyes watered from the stench. Her father didn't spare her a glance.

"My daughter is engaged to Reggie Larsen, boys. She wouldn't go near another man." His voice sounded so sure, Lilly was sickened to think he was about to be made a fool.

"You need to keep a shorter leash on her!" Clive stumbled forward and threw a bottle onto the porch. It smashed at her father's feet. He didn't even flinch.

"This here is a warnin'—you keep that girl of yours under lock and key and away from the enemy, or we'll teach her and your whole family a lesson in patriotism!" Clive curled his lip and spat on the ground. He waved at Lilly, who shrank behind her father. "I see you there, Missy. And I know what ya done. Your friend Henry is gonna git a reminder about keepin' his paws off American girls!"

Lilly went cold. Heinrick against Clive and three drunken brutes? She closed her eyes and buried her face in her father's back.

"Get outta here, boys." Her father's voice carried on the wind and must have seemed like thunder to the inebriated men because they spooked and backed up.

"You remember what we said, Missy! You stay home!"

As her father stood there, Lilly saw him as a lone wall of protection between a prejudiced world and his family. She was horrified to know she'd brought it on, but profoundly thankful for her father's courage. He was stoic as the four men rode off. Then he whirled, grabbed Lilly by her thin cotton-clothed arm, and marched her back into the house.

That's when she began to tremble.

twenty-two

"We'll clean up, then we'll talk." Her father's voice was tight.

Lilly instantly discovered untapped energy. She swept the broken glass and fastened the shutters. Her mother, Olive, and Bonnie worked silently beside her. Lilly shed noiseless tears as she watched her mother pile the broken china on the kitchen table. Bonnie occasionally frowned in her direction, but it was Olive's unmasked glare that made Lilly want to crawl under her bed and hide.

Finally, the house was put in order. Their mother sent Bonnie, DJ, and Frankie to their rooms. Olive stomped upstairs and slammed the door to her parents' bedroom. Lilly's mother sank into the willow rocker and folded her hands on her lap, her mouth a muted line. Her father ran his hand through his brown hair and paced in a circle near the sofa. Lilly knew he fought a swelling anger.

"What's this all about, Lilly?"

"I know what it's about!" Olive snarled from the top landing. A scarecrow in her white nightgown, fury blazed in Olive's dark eyes, and her face twisted in rage. She stormed down the stairs, waving a parchment envelope.

Lilly went numb. "Where did you get that?"

Olive ignored her. "It's a letter from him. From that German spy she met in town!"

Lilly clenched her teeth and glanced at her father. A muscle tensed in his jaw as he looked between his two daughters. He frowned at Lilly, and she shrank into a hard-backed chair.

Olive wore a crazed look. "You've been getting letters from him, haven't you? Letters from the enemy! You're a traitor! You've betrayed us all." She threw the letter at Lilly. It spiraled to the floor. Lilly ducked her head.

"Go to bed, Olive."

Olive recoiled from her father's command as if she'd been slapped. She stabbed a finger at Lilly. "She doesn't deserve Reggie."

Silence threw a thousand accusing jabs as Lilly weighed those words. Then Olive's wretched sobs broke the stunned quiet. She covered her face with her hands, and her body shook. Her father held her.

Lilly's heart twisted and tears flowed as she watched her sister suffer. She'd never meant to bring this kind of grief to her family.

Olive finally disentangled herself from her father's grasp. Without a glance at Lilly, she turned and climbed the stairs, every thump echoing through the house. Lilly heard her parents' bedroom door close.

Her father turned to her. His lips were pinched in suppressed fury. She sucked a deep breath and glanced at her mother, who offered her a slightly pitying look. Mr. Clark sat on the edge of the sofa, clasped his hands together, and raised his brows.

Lilly gulped. Then, working her fingers into knots, she spilled out the story. She started with the fight on the street, included the English lessons, the horseback ride, the butterfly comb, and her confrontation with Marjorie.

"But I didn't kiss him," Lilly insisted.

Her father shook his head. "You didn't have to—you already gave him your heart. That's betrayal enough."

Lilly caught her breath. He was right. She *had* given Heinrick her heart. And in doing so, she'd been unfaithful to Reggie. But they were all missing the most important part of her story.

"Father, Heinrick opened a door to God. Somehow, through his words, I saw that I feared God, as if He was a wolf waiting to eat me if I did something wrong. But Heinrick showed me that isn't true. God loves me and has a good plan for my life. And when I make mistakes or don't do everything right, I am still loved. Heinrick taught me how to trust God, no matter what happens. He showed me the keys to freedom, to joy, and God unlocked my prison."

Her father's face softened, and Lilly was relieved to see his anger dissolve. "Lilly," he said in his controlled bass, "you've cost this family a great deal this evening by your impulsiveness. You've shown bad judgment—"

"But what about—"

He held up a hand and silenced his daughter with a piercing look. "You're engaged to another man, Lilly. You've made a commitment to him, and you owe him your promise."

Lilly glanced at her mother. Her mother's eyes were wide, and she leaned forward in the rocker.

"I forbid you ever to see this Heinrick again, Lilly. You will stay home, and if you leave the house, you will be with Bonnie, Olive, or your parents." Her father lowered his voice. "When Reggie gets home, you will plead his forgiveness. And we will all hope and pray he forgives you and decides to marry you anyway."

Lilly felt as if he had slugged her. "Father, you can't want me to marry someone I don't love!"

He leaned back into the fraying sofa and put his wide weathered hands on his knees. "You do love Reggie, Lilly. You haven't seen him for over a year. You were lonely, and we can understand your vulnerability. But that's over. Reggie is coming home, and you'll see I'm right." His eyes kneaded her with a sudden tenderness, and Lilly's eyes filled with new tears. "Honey, I am doing this for you. For your own good." He glanced at his wife. "She'll thank me later."

Lilly couldn't look at her mother. Tears dripped off her chin, and she felt as if she'd just been dressed down like a six year old. She had less freedom than Frankie did. And her father was going to give her to a man she didn't love.

The realization hit her like a winter blast. She didn't love Reggie. How could that be? She'd grown up with him, practically worshiped him from the day he started teasing her at school. She thought he'd made her dreams come true when he asked her to marry him. Reggie was her life. How could she think she didn't love him?

But it was true. Somehow, she'd denied it, for how long she couldn't guess. Her feelings for Reggie were wrapped in a package of expectations, respect, and gratefulness. But Reggie couldn't make her heart soar. Only Heinrick could do that. Only Heinrick knew the real, unmasked Lilly, the afraid Lilly, the impulsive and even brave Lilly. He unearthed her innermost thoughts and embraced them with a touch of unconditional and breathtaking love. Lilly choked, feeling as if her father had tightened a noose around her neck. She had no choices. Trusting God, consulting Him, surrendering to His plans, whatever they were, were not a part of the equation. She had others to obey—her parents, Reggie.

Despair snuffed out the ember of hope that had burst into flame only earlier that evening.

Lilly hung her head. "Yes, Father."

&

Darkness hovered like a fog over the wheat field. Lilly sat in the window seat, her head in her folded arms, her eyes swollen. Her father had dismissed her to her room an hour prior, but sleep was forgotten in the mourning of her heart. She slouched in the windowsill and felt a numbing cold creep over her.

Lilly rose and tiptoed toward her closet. Maybe her father would allow her a brief trip to the river to watch the sunrise. She needed the fingers of light to weave into her soul; and the maple grove, despite the memories it stored of Heinrick, was also the place God had spoken to her and reminded her to seek Him. He promised she would find Him when she looked for Him. Even when she'd been bereft over the loss of Reggie, God had carried her. He could carry her now.

She changed into a brown wool dress and long stockings and grabbed her knit gray shawl as she padded from her room.

Lilly approached the landing and heard her parents' muffled voices from the family room below. They had not gone to bed, either. Guilt burned in her chest, but she couldn't keep her curiosity from planting herself on the top step. Their conversation became distinct as she held her breath and ignored her pounding heart.

"My father felt the same way," her mother was saying. "Don't you remember the night you asked him for my hand? He nearly broke his arm throwing you out of the house."

Lilly's heart lightened to hear her father's soft chuckle. Then his voice turned solemn. "This is different, Ruth. I wasn't a foreigner. The world wasn't at war."

"No, you were from a different church. And you were poor. To my parents, that was worse."

Lilly wrapped her arms around her knees and concentrated to catch every word.

"And what about her new faith, Donald? You can't say Reggie brought her that."

"Reggie is a good man. He loves God and will guide her spiritually."

Her mother's harrumph ricocheted up the stairs. "If Reggie's belief in God is anything like Pastor Larsen's, I think it is Lilly who will teach him."

"Now Ruth, Pastor Larsen is a wise man."

"Wise and firm. But is he kind? And what about Reggie? Will he treat Lilly with gentleness and love?"

"Of course he will. And he has a sound future in front of him. What kind of life can some German immigrant give her? Is that what we want for Lilly?"

"I don't think it's up to us, Donald. Lilly trusts us, but we need to let her make her own decisions."

"I'm her father. I have to look out for her."

Lilly sensed the texture of her mother's voice soften. She imagined her touching her husband softly on the arm, as was her habit. "Just like my father looked out for me and gave you a chance to prove your love. He knew I loved you, and he knew I thought God wanted me to marry you. So he waited in giving my hand until he was sure of the one God had chosen.

God's given me a good life with you, Dear. It may not have been an easy life, but it's been a joyful one."

Tears edged Lilly's eyes. She shouldn't be listening to their intimate conversation. She gathered herself to creep back to her room. But her father's last words burned in her ears.

"Ruth, you're a persuasive woman. If this fella can prove to me he loves her more than Reggie, I'll give him a chance."

Lilly stumbled to her room, stifling a cry. Her father would have let Heinrick prove himself! But it was too late. Heinrick had told her good-bye, and right now, he was probably lying in a pool of his own blood. Lilly threw herself on the bed next to Bonnie, curled into a ball, and wept.

twenty-three

"Get your paws off Christian," Olive snarled and turned her dark eyes on Lilly. Lilly slowly put the toddler back on the floor, where he'd been playing with a wooden spoon, and backed away from him. She avoided Olive's glare, but shuddered as she heard Olive slam a plate down at her place on the table. Olive acted as if Lilly's betrayal had singularly led to Chuck's death. It was more than a cold, aloof snubbing. Olive sizzled with hatred and was directing the blaze at Lilly.

Lilly felt like the apostle Paul, under Roman house arrest. She even envied the birds, the lark and crow, who scolded her, then lifted in flight over the prairie. What did their eyes see when they flew over the Torgesen T? Did they see Heinrick, well and hustling cattle? Or was he lying in a bunkhouse, bleeding, broken, near death? The horror of it assaulted her at odd times; while she hung laundry, when she dipped out water from the rain barrel, once when she milked the cows. And, despite her attempts to push the memory aside, she couldn't seem to escape the look of joy in his eyes when she told him she loved him.

Lilly mourned Heinrick in private, pouring out her tears late at night under cover of her quilt and praying for release from the grip of heartache. His magnetic blue eyes and tireless smile pressed against her, and there were times she felt crushed and thought she would break from the pain. Other times, the load seemed to lighten, as if some hand had lifted it from her heart. Lilly fought to put him out of her mind. From dawn to dusk, she buried herself in her chores, read her Bible, and hoped for dreamless, exhausted sleep. She relentlessly tried to believe her father's words—she'd simply been lonely and her feelings for Heinrick were built upon boredom.

But, as the days turned over into weeks and October blew the fire-lit leaves of ash and maples into the yard, she realized a part of Heinrick would always be hers. He'd left her his legacy, the imprint of the force that defined his life—a personal relationship with the Lord of the universe. The key to joy incarnate was Heinrick's gift to her. For that freedom, she would always be grateful she'd met him.

❧

Lilly altered her wedding dress, finishing it the first week of November. She embroidered, white upon the white satin, a floral pattern designed from her own drying lilies of the valley, with oversized bells that cascaded down the skirt from the sculptured empire waistline. She removed the sheer lace overskirt and added the lace instead to the elbow-length sleeves. The wide, wispy cuffs were contrary to popular styles, but they were exactly what she wanted. She hung the dress over the door of her wardrobe.

"Lilly, it's breathtaking." Her mother folded her arms and leaned against the doorframe.

Grateful, Lilly smiled.

Her mother drew Lilly into her arms. "You'll be a beautiful bride."

Lilly nodded into her mother's shoulder.

Her mother pulled away and held her at arm's length. "I know you had hoped for something different. . . ."

She forced a smile. "No, Mother. I'm ready to marry Reggie."

Mother Clark's brows arched.

"I know it's the right thing to do."

Her mother flattened her smile and nodded, as if understanding. She laid a hand on Lilly's shoulder and squeezed gently, and Lilly wished she'd spoken the truth.

❧

Lilly tucked her hair into a knit bonnet, pulled on a wool duster, and hustled out the door. Her family, minus Olive and Christian, were already headed into town.

Minutes ago, a rider on horseback had galloped through their yard, leaving in his wake the triumphant announcement—the Germans had surrendered to the Allied Forces somewhere in the middle of the French wilds. The war was over. Lilly watched the messenger tear north, toward the Torgesen T, and wondered how the news would greet Heinrick. He was no longer the enemy. She shoved the thought aside and caught up to her family. It didn't matter, anyway. Reggie would surely be home soon.

In town, forgiveness drifted on the crisp winter air. Mrs. Larsen, who had heretofore regarded Lilly with frigid eyes and an acid tongue, wrapped her in a two-armed hug and squeezed. "Now we can all get back to our lives," she whispered.

Main Street was packed, and Miller's did a thriving coffee and tea business while selling copies of the Armistice telegram that had sped across the country. Bonnie skipped down the steps of the pharmacy, waving the surrender details. Huddling next to her mother and listening as her father read the account, Lilly spied Marjorie standing in a clump of ecstatic women. Lilly tightened her jaw and ignored the stab in her heart.

The train whistle blew. Lilly took a deep breath and wondered if today, finally, she would receive word from Reggie. She had no address for him, had no idea where to send her own half-written scripts. But she didn't know what to say, either. They would have to sort it out when he came home, if he came home.

The train pulled into the station and coughed. The echo of it carried across town. Lilly made a mental note to check her box later.

She leaned forward and listened to her father finish the newspaper story. Her mother patted her hand. "Praise God, it's over."

Lilly could only nod. Finally, Mobridge could regroup, collectively mourn its losses, and rebuild. The community could patch the wounds, lay to rest the fears and the horror, and stumble forward into the future. Lilly knew they would find a way to hold onto the land, their legacies, and their love. They would survive.

A gasp washed like a wave through the clusters of gossiping townspeople. Lilly bristled, and an odd sensation rippled up her spine. She looked up and went weak.

"Hello, Lilly." Reggie stood in the middle of the street, his khaki uniform wrinkled under an open overcoat, his dress cap tilted crazily over his hand, and a sprig of short black hair sticking out like a flagpole over his eyes. He smiled a smooth milky grin. He leaned forward, as if she hadn't heard him, and repeated himself. "Lilly?"

Lilly cried out and rushed toward his open arms.

Mrs. Larsen beat her to him. She clung to her son and wept. Reggie buried his head in his mother's neck and held her.

Lilly stood paralyzed. She waited, watching the wind toy with his hat, then knock it aloft. It fingered his short hair, lifted the collar of his coat, and carried to her the smell of wool and perspiration, confidence and strength. The smell of Reggie. She breathed in deeply.

Reggie finally extracted himself from his sobbing mother and stepped toward Lilly. She met his eyes and saw buried in them a thousand battles, not all with guns and bombs. Reggie reached out and slipped his hand around her neck. He paused, then in a desperate moment, drew her against him, burying his face in her hair. "Lilly," he groaned. "I feared I would never see you again."

She encircled his waist with her arms and pulled him close. They embraced while a hundred eyes watched them, measuring, considering. Lilly knew this was probably their last untarnished moment. Once his mother had him alone, she could reveal to him the indiscretions of his disobedient fiancée. If not her, then Marjorie, Ernestine, or even Olive. Somehow, the tale would emerge, and the unwavering trust between them that had been theirs before the war and now, in this magical moment, would be forever scarred. She clutched him tighter.

"You missed me," he said, his voice husky.

Lilly pulled back and stared into his wounded brown eyes. She felt the pricking of tears and nodded. A grin tugged at his mouth. "And I missed you."

Then he lowered his face and kissed her. It felt familiar and warm.

Reggie finally released her, pinned on her one last meaningful look, and then stepped into the multitude. Lilly let free a shuddering, cleansing breath. Hope had returned to the prairie in vivid intensity.

Mrs. Larsen pulled at Lilly's arm, her face close. "We'll be up tomorrow to discuss wedding plans."

Lilly nodded and saw Reggie disappear into the crowd.

❧

That night, as she and Bonnie were undressing for bed, Bonnie stole up behind her and placed a small parchment envelope on her vanity. Lilly stared at it and blanched. "Where did you get it?"

Bonnie looked at her, curiosity in her youthful eyes. "I picked it up at the post office today."

Lilly fingered the envelope and examined the bold, block letters. Her skin prickled.

"Is it from him?"

Lilly shot her sister a glance.

Bonnie shrugged and smiled mysteriously. "Sometimes you talk in your sleep."

Lilly swallowed hard.

Bonnie giggled. "Don't worry. Your secret is safe with me."

What secret? Lilly turned over the envelope in her hands and cautiously worked it open.

Short and dated the first week of October, the note made her tremble.

Dear Lilly,

I heard about your home, and I am sorry for the trouble I caused you. The Torgesens have released me from my contract,

and I am leaving Mobridge. Thank you for your friendship; you
are written upon my heart. The words from Ruth 2:12 speak
my hope for you. May the good Lord repay you for your kindness.
May He protect you and reward you. Go with God, Lilly.

Yours,
Heinrick

Lilly moaned and clutched the letter to her chest. He was gone, and somehow, with him, went the last shred of a love that had seemed so intoxicating, so breathtaking, so encompassing. And so right.

Lilly fell to her knees, buried her head into the crazy quilt, and sobbed. Bonnie knelt beside her and rubbed her back.

Why, on the day of Reggie's return, when peace should finally be hers, did she feel as though she were back in battle?

twenty-four

"I think we'll have a Thanksgiving wedding." Reggie tucked his hands in the pocket of his woolen gray duster and peered into Lilly's eyes. Sheltered in the grove of maples, the howl of the unrelenting wind didn't seem as loud and menacing. Lilly folded her mittened hands together and nodded, an acquiescing smile on her face. Two weeks seemed a mere blink away, but she'd been waiting for two years. The sooner it happened, the better.

Reggie studied her. "You've changed, Lilly. You seem, oh, I don't know, more serious. I expected my bubbly, carefree Lilly." His eyes clouded. "You seem pensive."

Lilly bit her lip.

Reggie turned away and propped up his collar. "You aren't even happy to see me."

Lilly's heart twisted. She put a hand on his arm. "Of course I am."

He turned and considered her a long moment. It seemed to Lilly he seemed shorter, not quite as towering as he'd been. And his dark eyes were sharper, older. His face was lean, his angled jaw cleanly shaven. She'd observed him all week, especially today at morning service, and noted he carried an unfamiliar air of wariness that could only be reaped by war. And once, when she'd slid her hand onto his arm while he gazed across the frost-covered fields, he'd nearly jumped out of his skin. His eyes brimmed with anger, and it took him a full painful five seconds to tuck some horrific moment into the folds of memory. But the residue of hatred frightened her.

Reggie pulled away from her touch and stalked out to the bluff. The breeze blew through his short hair. He stared across the river. "In France, this view was all I could think of.

Home. Being with you. It seemed the only reason worth fighting. Whenever the commander yelled for us to attack and the blood froze in my veins, the thought of you waiting for me gave me the courage to climb over the barricades. One step at time, one shot at a time, I figured I was headed home."

Tears welled in Lilly's eyes. She edged toward him. "Why didn't you write? It's been three months since your telegram." Her voice cracked. "What happened?"

Reggie's voice hardened. "I couldn't write because I couldn't see. Some nurse sent the telegram for me." Rawness, as though the incident had happened yesterday, entered his tone. "I was hit by mustard gas the day Harley and Chuck were killed." He paused and drew in a deep breath. "Luckily, I shoved on my mask right after it hit, so I didn't get the worst of it. Instead, I saw my best buddies killed." Grief twisted his face. Lilly tugged on his arm and led him to a bleached cottonwood. He sat and hung his head in his hands.

Lilly tucked herself beside him.

"It was horrible. I couldn't breathe. After the fighting stopped, we crawled out of our bunkers and took off our masks. Then the torture began. My eyes felt as if they had been seared with a branding torch. They glued together, and my throat closed. It swelled up, and I couldn't swallow. I was choking."

Tears chilled Lilly's cheeks.

Reggie's voice dropped. "They had to strap me down."

Lilly gazed across the ice-edged river and conjured up a ghastly image of Reggie tied to a hospital bed. She felt ill and longed to close her ears to his words.

"All I could think of the entire time was you, Lilly. You and our future."

Lilly wrapped her arms around herself, pushing against physical pain.

Reggie turned to her. "I don't want to wait until Thanksgiving. I would marry you tomorrow if I could. I just want to get back to some kind of normalcy, the life I always dreamed of." He wrapped her upper arms in an iron grip and turned her to face him. "Please, say you will marry me, Lilly."

His brown eyes probed hers, and Lilly saw in them desperation and longing so intense, she knew she couldn't deny him. She couldn't cause him more pain. "Of course I will, Reggie."

He pulled her to himself and kissed her, powerfully, winding his arm around her neck and holding her tight.

&

Lilly fled into her wedding plans. Somehow, tucked inside Reggie's grins and Mrs. Larsen's babbling, Lilly felt a measure of calm, as if she'd negotiated a cease-fire in her heart. She marched forward, toward the inevitable conclusion, and told herself this was right.

But tiny sputters of doubt began to explode deep inside her heart.

"I saw Erica Torgesen in town today," commented Reggie as they sat together on the porch steps, bundled and staring at the hazy sputter of the sun.

Lilly peered at him sideways.

"She asked if you had time to sew her something for the New Year's social." He gave her a stern eye, his mouth a firm line. "I took the liberty of telling her you wouldn't be doing that sort of thing anymore."

Lilly looked past him, north toward the Torgesen T, and said nothing.

Sunday, after church, Reggie closed in during the walk home. "Mother told me you haven't been attending the Ladies Aid meetings." His hand seemed rough on her arm. "I thought we agreed you would help with tea, Lilly."

She shot him a frown. Did she agree to help? Or had Reggie and Mrs. Larsen consented for her?

Lilly beat back the flames of doubt, however, with prayer and a patient spirit. She was just nervous, as any bride would be. She clung to the faith that God had her future in His hands and would lead her to a lifetime of joy. God would give her peace as she walked forward in faith. She just had to be patient.

Snow peeled from the clouds in soft translucent layers and melted on the hard-packed road. Lilly meandered toward Mobridge, her hands tucked in a beaver skin muff, occasionally catching a few flakes on her tongue and nose. The sun was a glittering pumpkin, brilliant against a silver gray sky and frosting the bluffs orange.

Lilly sighed and picked up her pace. She was already late, expected by Mrs. Larsen and the others on the Ladies Aid committee to help decorate the church. Her family would join her in an hour or so, Olive and her mother each toting the Clark family's contribution to the Thanksgiving pie social—pumpkin and apple pies.

Next year she would be appearing with Mrs. Larsen, toting her own pie, as Reggie's wife. Reggie had already prepared a room for them at the Larsen home while he readied himself to take on a congregation of his own. He mentioned a year of preparation while he worked with his father and learned the "trade." Lilly had considered, with the anger that bubbled out occasionally when he mentioned Chuck, Harley, the Germans, or anything that had to do with the Great War, it might take him longer to find the peace to minister to others. But she'd clamped her mouth shut after he told her it was none of her business and asked how she could possibly understand his nightmares. So, she determined to find a way to live in the Larsen household until she could create one of her own.

Mrs. Larsen was thrilled to have another helping hand around the house and told her so.

The town was barren; the shops closed, customary on the day before Thanksgiving. Lilly heard the train whistle skip along the frozen prairie in the distance and recalled the days when she would race the wind to greet the mail train with a letter. It was a time of innocence and naive hopes, a lifetime apart from what she knew now—the reality, and cost, of love.

She rounded the armory and was passing Miller's when

she spotted him. She almost didn't recognize the man, dressed in a pair of forest green woolen pants and a knee-length matching wool coat—standard issue brakeman's uniform for the Milwaukee Road. He could have been any other railroad man, toting a lead lantern, headed for work. But he wasn't. She knew him the minute her gaze traveled upward and took in the long blond hair trickling out in curls from his wool railroad cap.

"Heinrick," she breathed into the wind. He whirled and saw her.

He paused, as if determining the distance between them, in so many ways, then turned and strode toward her. As he drew closer, she reached out her hand. He caught it in his and purposefully led her to the small alley between Bud's and the armory, where they had nearly kissed and been discovered. Where her heart had entwined hopelessly and forever with his.

Heinrick set down his lantern and glanced into the empty street. He released her hand, gripped her upper arms, and pinned his eyes to hers. "Lilly."

Lilly's breath caught. She heard in his raw tone and saw in his eyes what she hoped for—a longing for her, a missing so intense it was etched into his heart.

"Are you all right?" she whispered.

He cracked a crooked grin, and Lilly's heart thumped.

"I'm all right."

Three words, and yet with them, fear broke free and relief crested over her. Her voice shook. "I've been so worried, Heinrick. Clive said he was going to hurt you, teach you a lesson."

Heinrick closed his eyes and nodded. "Well, he tried, that's for sure." Then he opened his eyes and they twinkled with a familiar mischief. "But, those boys never fought a man who worked shoveling sand ten hours a day. Besides, Erica Torgesen doesn't like roughhousing, and she put it to Clive to either let me go or leave me be."

Lilly squinted at him, noting an unfamiliar scar above his

left eye. She wondered what he wasn't telling her. Lilly arched her brows. "So Clive let you go?"

"*Ja*. Did you get my note?"

Lilly nodded.

"I wrote it after I got my job on the line. I was passing through here and dropped it off."

Heinrick looked away. "I have bad timing."

Lilly frowned, then remembered the day she'd received his letter. The day Reggie came home.

"You saw Reggie."

Heinrick's mouth was pinched, and when he looked at her, hurt ringed his eyes. "I'm very happy for you, Lilly."

Lilly's eyes misted.

"I'm stationed in Sioux Falls, now. I just stopped in today to pick up some gear I had in storage." He nodded to a rucksack on his back.

He bent to grab his lantern, as if intending to say goodbye and walk out of her life forever.

"Heinrick, wait." Lilly stepped toward him, not really knowing what she wanted to say, but realizing she had to say something, anything to keep him there long enough for her to know. . . .

Heinrick paused and looked down at her, almost wincing. He reached for a rebellious strand of hair that had loosened from her bonnet and rubbed its softness between his fingers.

"Lilly, I can't take you away from Reggie. You have to choose, on your own. You have to come to me freely. Because if you don't, you'll be exchanging one prison for another."

He dropped her hair, ran his finger along her jaw, then lifted her chin. "More than that, you must do what God wants you to do."

Lilly opened her mouth, and her thoughts spilled out. "But I don't know what that is."

Heinrick considered her a long moment. "Have you asked Him and really listened for the answer?"

Lilly gave him a blank look while her mind sifted through

his question. He was right. She'd never seriously listened to God's answer, never considered any reply but the one she already knew.

But it was too late to change course. Her wedding was two days away. She shook her head.

Heinrick's jaw stiffened. "Then I can't make your decision for you." The train whistle screamed as it pulled into the station. "I have to go, Lilly. May God bless your marriage." He turned away.

Lilly put a hand on his arm and folded her fingers into the wool. "I have to know, Heinrick." Her tone betrayed her heart.

He frowned.

"Do you love me?"

His mouth curved wryly, and she thought she saw a flicker of sadness in his stormy blue eyes. He covered her hand with his own. "I've loved you since the day you saved me on the street."

"I thought you said you didn't need any help."

His voice turned raw. "I needed help, Lilly. I needed, more than anything, for someone to walk beside me, to be my friend and encourage me to fight for a place in this country." He touched her cheek. "God sent you to do that for me. And now, because of you, I have a future here." His gaze lingered on her, and she felt the strength of his feelings sweep through her.

Then, he snatched the lantern and strode away. And, with each long step, Lilly knew he was taking with him her heart.

twenty-five

Lilly headed for the cloakroom and pulled off her coat. Mechanical. Steadfast. Resolute. She walked into the sanctuary and presented herself for service. Alice Larsen shot her a scowl. Lilly ignored it.

The pews in the small sanctuary were pushed back against the walls, creating a large square gap in the center. Two cloth-covered tables lined the center of the room, a throne for the pies.

Ernestine put her to work lighting candles. Lilly glanced out a window. Pellet-sized snowflakes fell from the darkening sky and covered the fields in a thick blanket. Families began to stream in, pies gathering on the two tables. Lilly smiled, nodded, and greeted.

Her mother and Olive arrived and added their pies to the table. Bonnie peeled layers of wraps off DJ and Frankie. Her father came in, a film of crystalline snow on his wool jacket. "We're in for it, folks," he commented wryly.

Rev. Larsen offered Mr. Clark his hand. "Nothing like the winter of 1910, though. It started snowing in June that year and didn't let up 'til the following July!"

Lilly's father guffawed and pumped the preacher's arm.

Lilly slid up to the two men. "Excuse me, Reverend. Do you know where Reggie is?"

Rev. Larsen raised his eyebrows. "Lost track of him already, Lilly? And you aren't even married yet!" He eyed her father, who smirked.

Lilly blushed. Rev. Larsen put a hand on her shoulder. "He rode out earlier with Clive Torgesen and some of the other boys, hunting pheasants. He'll be here."

The crowd thickened quickly. The Thanksgiving pie feast

was akin to the fair in terms of pie competition. Everyone had a favorite. Lilly favored Jennifer Pratt's vanilla crème. She surveyed the crowd but didn't find either Marjorie or the Pratt family.

Rev. Larsen led them in a time of Thanks-sharing, then the pies were attacked. DJ and Frankie grabbed their favorites, a tart crabapple from the Ed Miller family and a fresh peach from Ernestine's, which Willard admitted he'd made. Lilly accepted a bite of each, but wasn't hungry for her own. Her thoughts were occupied with a still missing Reggie, and Heinrick.

The crowd began to scatter, the adults bundling up the children for the ride home.

"Coming with us, Lilly?" Her mother's voice carried over the room as she tugged DJ's cap over his ears.

Lilly shook her head. "No. I'll wait for Reggie."

Her father looked worried. "Don't stay out too long, Lilly. That storm is whippin' up."

Lilly helped clear tables with the Ladies Aid, but avoided the women when they clumped in gossip. The wind outside began to moan, but it drew her to the church entrance. Perhaps a blast of cold air could untangle the knot in her heart. Pulling on her coat, she cracked the door open and slipped outside. The wind encircled her, groaning in her ears, and pawing at her coat. She stuck her hands in the pockets and wrapped it around her.

Instinctively, her hand closed around an object in the well of her pocket. She pulled it out and her heart tumbled. Heinrick's butterfly comb. She turned over the exquisite gift, and the dull, throbbing wound in her heart ripped open.

How had it landed in her pocket? She shifted through memory and found the day when she'd pulled it from her drawer and tried it on. The ginger-colored wings illuminated the few gold threads in her hair, and Lilly had left it in as she read her Bible that morning. She'd lost herself in the Beatitudes and completely forgotten the butterfly comb until she made ready to run into town with Bonnie for supplies. The comb had tangled in her wool bonnet. She'd pulled it off and slipped it into her coat pocket.

Tears welled in her eyes. Heinrick had given her a gift of his heritage. To complement her gift to him—his future.

"What are you doing out here, Lillian?" Mrs. Larsen's crisp tone scattered Lilly's thoughts. Mrs. Larsen yanked Lilly inside and shut the door behind her. "What's the matter with you, are you trying to make yourself sick?" The older woman pushed her toward the sanctuary.

Lilly bit the inside of her mouth and tried in vain to conceal her tears. But they spilled out. Mrs. Larsen looked at her, her brow puckered. "Reggie will be fine, Dear."

Lilly watched her pinched, soon-to-be mother-in-law join a group of cackling women and suddenly knew only one thing: She couldn't marry Reggie. She couldn't spend the rest of her life living a halfhearted love. She whirled and made for the door.

The door shuddered open just as she laid a hand on the latch. Reggie caught her as she stumbled forward.

"Where're you goin'?"

Her breath left her, and words locked in her mouth.

"You weren't going to wait for me?" Reggie's dark brows folded together. "What's this?" He snatched the comb from her hand. Turning it over, he examined it. His face darkened. "Where did you get this?"

Lilly balled her hands in her coat pockets. He looked at her, read her face. Then gave a sharp intake of breath, as if he'd been stabbed. He stared at her, shaking. "So it's true, then."

Her eyes widened.

"I know all about it, Lilly." His face tightened into a glare. "I know all about how you disgraced me, how you *kissed* another man, a German."

She saw the hate pulsing in his eyes, and her mouth went dry. She shuffled back into the church foyer. *Help me, Lord.*

"No, Reggie. You don't understand—"

Reggie hurled the comb out into the darkness. Then he stepped inside and pulled the door shut. The world seemed suddenly, intensely, still.

Lilly's pulse roared in her ears.

Reggie sucked a deep breath. He spoke quietly, through clenched teeth. "I can't believe you betrayed me with a German! If you were going to be unfaithful, couldn't you have chosen an American?"

Lilly's knees shook. "I'm sorry, Reggie."

Reggie must have detected her fear, for his glower softened, leaving only cool, stony eyes. He backed Lilly into the wall, put a hand over her shoulder, and leaned close. She felt his hot breath on her face and couldn't move. He seemed to be making an effort to keep his voice calm. "Listen, Lilly, I'm willing to marry you anyway. Because you're mine and all I've ever wanted."

She fixed her eyes at the snow melting on his shoes, not wanting to speak the truth. But she owed him honesty. She'd never sent the letter she'd written explaining everything, so he didn't know. Didn't know the painful news about Heinrick, yes, but he also didn't know about the joy and life she'd found. He didn't know that God could change the plans, and everything could still turn out all right, even better, for both of them.

She summoned her courage. "But I don't know if that's what God wants," she said softly.

He took it like a blow and recoiled. "What?"

"I don't know if I am supposed to marry you, Reggie. I don't know if that is what God wants. I, we've, never really asked Him."

Reggie frowned at her. "Of course not! We don't have to ask God whom we're to marry. We just decide what we want, and if we do it right, He blesses us. God doesn't care whom we marry. He just wants us to go to church, to obey His commandments, to do what is right."

"I think He does care. I think He cares so much that if we don't ask Him, it's a sin."

Reggie blew out an exasperated breath. "Lilly, what do you know? I'm the one who is going to be a pastor." He looked at her steadily. "I want you. That's enough for me. Even though you betrayed me. Doesn't that prove my love for you?"

Confusion rocked her. Reggie's love felt constricting, suffocating—so different from Heinrick's.

"I don't need God's blessing to marry you."

Lilly raised wide eyes, thunderstruck. Embedded in Reggie's words, she discovered what was missing from their future, their plans, and her heart. She realized why her soul had never been, could never be, at peace about her marriage to Reggie. She didn't feel God's blessing.

"I. . .I can't marry you right now," Lilly stated in a faltering voice. "I have to wait on God. I have to know what He wants. Because I know He loves me, I want His plans for my life."

Reggie pounded his chest and stared at her, desperation punctuating his voice. "*I'm* His plan for your life!" He raked a hand through his snow-crusted hair. "Maybe Mother was right. I should have picked Marjorie." His expression darkened. "At least she would have been faithful."

Lilly felt a cold fist squeeze her heart.

Reggie's voice turned wretched. "But I chose you. You were the one I wanted. I've been planning this for years." He punched the wall behind her. Lilly trembled. "It isn't fair, Lilly. I've been through hell itself, and I return to find that someone's stolen my girl?"

Reggie's voice curdled in pain. Lilly closed her eyes felt ill. He was right. This wasn't what he deserved. But they couldn't base their marriage, the rest of their lives, on pity.

"It wasn't like that," Lilly said evenly. She opened her eyes. "Heinrick didn't steal me. But you're right. It isn't fair. Not to you—or me!" She thumped her own chest. "I found something, Reggie. I found God. I found freedom and joy." Her voice slowed. "And maybe that's how God wanted it. Maybe He wanted to give us some distance so we could see He had something better for us. That's how it's supposed to be, I think. His will and not ours, and that's better, even when it doesn't make sense."

Reggie buried his head in his forearm. "This can't be God's will. God wouldn't take you away from me. Don't throw our lives, my life, away."

He drew back and fixed her with a desperate intensity, as if, by his gaze, he could control her bizarre thinking. "Lilly, listen, you belong to me. You don't have a choice."

Lilly put a hand on her chest and pushed back an odd panic. "I do have a choice. You can't force me to love you. If you make me marry you, it still doesn't mean I'll love you. Love can't be forced or, for that matter, earned. It has to be a free gift. Like God's love for us, and ours for Him."

Reggie looked away. "He doesn't deserve our love."

Lilly winced at his words. She understood all too well. He believed God had let him down in leading him somewhere dark and painful.

"He *does* deserve our love, Reg, because He loved us first. He saved us when we didn't deserve it—still don't! But He loves us anyway. And we have to trust Him. We count on His love and His strength, and we surrender to His will. Because if we don't, I think we can never have peace."

"We get peace by obeying. By doing what we know is right. We don't have to ask; it's all written out for us."

Lilly leaned her head against the wall and sighed.

Reggie looked at her, his eyes narrowing. "I don't know what you think God wants, but I know this, Lilly. If you don't tell me right now you will marry me, then I don't want you."

She gaped at him and saw years of careful planning melt in the heat of his fury.

"I can't say yes," she whispered. "Not until I'm sure we have God's blessing, and right now, I don't know."

Reggie crossed his arms over his chest and stepped back. His face was granite, and he said nothing.

Lilly muffled a small cry as the reality of her words hit her. She ran past him, threw open the door, and flung herself into the swelling blizzard. Scrambling away from the church, she ran everywhere and nowhere and straight into the blindness and pain of her surrender. Though faint and swallowed by the moan of the wind, Lilly thought she heard a voice trail her. "Lilllyyyy!"

twenty-six

Lilly hugged her body and ducked her head against the snarling wind. Under the coal black sky, Lilly couldn't even discern her feet. She shivered as snow gathered on her neck.

She had no idea how far she'd run. But her feet were numb, and she shivered violently. She felt the fool. She'd plunged not only into the blizzard, but also into a life without Reggie, without the plans of her family or her church.

"What am I doing, Lord?"

The wind roared and spun her. She stumbled, then pitched forward. The snow climbed into her sleeves, layered her chin. She realized over a foot had accumulated. Lost and in the middle of a Dakota blizzard, she felt panic crest over her. "O God, help me!"

Climbing to her feet, she whacked the snow out of her sleeves. She tucked her hands into her pockets, wiggled her chin into her coat, and struggled forward. Her hair felt crusty and the wind whined in her ears. Lilly heaved one foot in front of the other, no longer able to feel the swells and ruts of the prairie landscape.

The bodily struggle felt easier than the war she waged against the angry voices in her head. She fought to filter through them, to hear only one. *What is Your will, Lord?*

If she'd asked earlier and had the courage to listen and obey, maybe she wouldn't be stumbling in the cold darkness.

She could no longer feel her legs. They seemed like sticks, and, at times, she wondered if she were truly moving or merely standing still. She was so tired; she just wanted to close her eyes. Couldn't she just rest a moment? Her ears burned, her hair was frozen, and her head throbbed.

She hit something head on, and it knocked her on her

backside. *Lord, is this it? Will I die because of my impulsiveness?* She rolled to all fours, gritted her teeth, and reached through the darkness. Her hand banged against something solid. She traced it upward and discovered metal at head height. A handle. Sliding her wrist around it, she heaved it open.

The smell of hay and manure had never been so sweet. Lilly crawled inside, feeling the heat of barn animals warm her face and filter through her clothing. She heard the snuffing of hay, the low of a cow. Fumbling forward, she bumped into a bucket of water, tipping it over. The water doused her hands and knees and felt like fire against her skin. Lilly pulled herself to her feet, knees quaking. Her head spun multi-colors. Groaning, she shuffled the length of the barn, clasping the stalls with her stinging hands until she discovered a mound of hay stacked in an empty paddock. Collapsing into it, she clawed out a hole. Then she climbed inside and curled into a ball. She knew she shouldn't sleep, but, oh, how sleep called her name, moving over her slowly, laying like a blanket upon her eyelids.

Lilly blew on her hands. *Thank You, Lord, for this place.* She tucked her legs under her coat. She must stay awake. She recalled stories of victims who had succumbed to sleep and frozen under a mound of crusted snow. Sleep was her enemy.

If she could stay awake, she was safe for the moment. But a much larger storm lurked outside the barn doors. Eventually they would find her, discover what she'd done, how she'd hurt Reggie. Then what? Heinrick was gone. Even if she could somehow find him and declare her love, what kind of life would that be? Outcasts, shunned by her family, her community. Living life as strangers in some foreign town. Lilly shook her head as if to exorcise the images. Besides, was Heinrick God's choice for her?

She kept returning to the lack of the blessing for which her soul seemed to scream. And what had her mother said so long ago? Marriage was too difficult for halfhearted commitment.

And something else about missing out on the fullness of joy God had planned for her.

Lilly buried her face in her hands. *Lord, what should I do? What do You want for me?* She closed her eyes and listened, aching to discern an audible voice. But the only things she heard were echoes, impressions from things she'd read, illustrations from Matthew about Jesus, the way He reached out in love, extreme in His pursuing of the people who rejected Him. They clung instead to the law, to an old way that would lead to death, most certainly beyond the grave, but in large part to death in life, also. A death of joy, a death of an exhilarating relationship with Christ.

Reggie was that death. That thought became the one clear beacon in her sleep-fogged mind. Reggie was the law. He clung to a religion that created laws that led to salvation rather than a salvation that led to obedience. It was a stagnant, suffocating, demoralizing religion. And it had been hers as well.

Until Heinrick introduced her to a God who loved her enough to die for her, when she was the most wretched of sinners, then gave her the choice to respond to Him in love. It was the ultimate love affair. Love given, not demanded. Love offered unconditionally.

Suddenly she knew she could never be trapped inside the circle of suffocation again. Better to fling herself out into an unknown dark blizzard and into the arms of her Savior than cling to a life that threatened to choke her.

Even if she could never see Heinrick again, even if he wasn't God's choice for her, she knew she could never return to the law, to Reggie. The resolve deepened with every warming heartbeat.

The straw crunched as she settled deeper into her well. She took a cleansing breath. She'd asked God and listened, and the Almighty had answered clearly.

She would wait for His choice, His blessing. One day at a time, she would surrender to His plans. She would ask, seek, and find. And she would live in the fullness of joy.

The door at the end of the barn rattled, groaned, and then pushed inward. The snow screamed as it entered, rolled around the startled animals, and ushered in a figure wrapped in wool. Lilly bolted upright. Her heart hammered as she peered through the padding of darkness.

The hooded figure raised a massive lead lantern, glowing blue from one of its brilliant orbs. It cast eerie gray shadows off the haystacks and caught the cows wide-eyed. "Lilly?"

Perhaps she was already asleep, and this was a dream. "Heinrick?"

He swung the lamp toward her voice, his feet crunching cold, stiff hay. From his muffler dripped a layer of snowy diamonds, and his eyebrows stuck out in frosty spikes. His blue eyes, however, blazed.

"Over here." Lilly's heart thundered as she fought to believe her eyes.

Heinrick closed the gap in two giant steps. "Oh, thank You, Lord." He set the lantern down, dropped to his knees, and reached out his frosted arms. He pulled her to his chest and tucked her head under his chin. His heart banged in his strong chest, and she felt relief shudder out of him. He held her long enough to betray the depth of his worry.

When he released her, he pulled off his gloves and clutched her face with his icy hands. "Are you all right?" He looked her over, head to toe.

Lilly closed her eyes and nodded.

"*Ja*, but you are freezing!" Heinrick peeled off his coat.

"How did you find me?"

He tucked the coat around her. "By the grace of God, Lilly." He dusted the last snow off the collar and avoided her eyes.

Lilly squinted at him. "I thought you left town. What happened?"

"The train got snowed in." He began to knock down hay. "I was headed toward Fannie's when I saw you run out into the storm." The hay fell in quiet rustles around her. He worked steadily, mutely, and she knew something was amiss. Had he heard her fight with Reggie? Heinrick didn't stay quiet unless he was fighting a battle. Then he was a man of few words and a set jaw.

She watched him build a tiny castle of insulation. The heat from Heinrick's coat was warming her with the effect of a roaring fire. But the fact he'd found her in the middle of a whiteout heated her from the inside out. This had to be her answer, her audible voice. Just like the voice calling through the mists of the battlefield in her dream, Heinrick had searched through a blizzard for her. Loving him would cost her everything, but as she embraced the idea, the fragrance of peace was so intense, she gasped.

Heinrick was God's answer. He'd been trying to tell her for months. From the moment Heinrick had nearly run her over with a mustang, to the day he sent her the note committing her to the Lord, God had written Heinrick on her heart and filled her mind with his voice. Only Heinrick loved her the way God wanted a husband to love—unconditionally, fully, and sacrificially. Only Heinrick pointed her to the Savior.

Heinrick crawled inside his fortress, then threaded an arm around her and pulled her against his muscled chest. "We'll stay here until the storm breaks. Then I'll take you home."

"I am home." Lilly tilted her head to look at him.

Heinrick considered her, his arched brows like a drift of fine snow. "Lilly, you're cold and confused. I saw you run from the church, and I saw Reggie standing in the door. You had a fight, that's all. Things will look better after the storm blows over."

"I am home, Heinrick," Lilly repeated emphatically. "Home is where God puts you. It's being with those you love. It's where you have peace, remember?"

Heinrick gave her a slow nod.

"I have peace with you. I think *you* are my home."

A rueful grin slid onto Heinrick's face. "But I am the

enemy, Lilly. A foreigner."

Lilly put a hand on his cold, whiskered face. "Do you remember your last note? You quoted Ruth, when she made the ultimate act of commitment. Let me finish it for us." Lilly closed her eyes and paraphrased, "Don't urge me to leave you or turn back from you. Your people will be my people, and your God my God."

Heinrick placed his hand over hers. It belonged there. "And you will be blessed because you left your home and traveled to a foreign land."

"Ya," Lilly said.

Heinrick winced at her terrible German impression. Then, growing serious, his intentions pooled in his eyes for a second time. He ran a finger under her chin; she lifted her face to his and let him kiss her. It was gentle, lingering, and full of promise.

Lilly pulled away, her eyes wide, and saw that his own were dancing. "You do love me."

"*Ja*, my Lilly, I love you." He kissed her again, and she knew she had never loved Reggie like she loved this man.

Suddenly, she pulled away and groaned. "Heinrick, what about my parents? I told Reggie I didn't want to marry him. I told him I had to wait until I knew what God wanted, until I had His blessing. But I can't get married without my parents' blessing, either."

Heinrick caressed her face. "And do you know what God wants? Do you have His blessing?"

"Yes."

His eyes glowed with an unmistakable passion. "Jacob worked fourteen years for the woman he loved, and it seemed to him but a moment for his love for her. I am a patient man. I will wait until I am no longer the enemy."

Then he leaned back, the straw protesting, and nestled her against his chest. She warmed and eventually slept. He held her until the sun rose and chased away the irate wind and kissed the fields with tiny golden sparkles.

"See, the prairie is the ocean," said Lilly as Heinrick helped her through waves of crested snow.

Heinrick laughed. "I crossed it, my sweet Lilly, to find you."

epilogue

They had planned a Thanksgiving Day wedding, and when Lilly awoke that morning and saw the pink beads of dawn glinting off the snow-blanketed fields in heavenly magnificence, she knew Heinrick was right. Thanksgiving was the perfect day to commit their lives to one another; after all, it was a celebration of God's grace and salvation after a season of struggle. Lilly counted it as a miracle that it had taken only a year for her father to consent to their marriage.

"Are you ready?" Bonnie asked. Lilly glanced at her sister, whose joy was evident in her teenage smile and dancing eyes. Lilly nodded. She cast one last look at the prairie from the window seat in her bedroom. Giant waves of snow, halted in mid crest, leaped across the fields, the sun's rays glancing off them like a golden mist. It was glorious, the aftermath of a Dakotan blizzard. The contrast between the fury and the calm never ceased to amaze her, just like peace that filled her heart after a difficult surrender.

Lilly felt a warm hand on her shoulder. She turned, and her mother's gentle eyes were on her. "He's waiting," she said softly, a smile tugging at her lips.

Lilly stood, brushed off her slip, and stepped into the wedding gown her sister held. A twinge of regret stabbed her; she wished Marjorie were here. But her friend's wounds were deep, and Lilly knew healing would be long in coming. Lilly's prayers for Marjorie were constant, as were her prayers for Reggie. She hadn't seen him since the night of the fateful blizzard a year ago and heard he'd left to find his fortune in the Black Hills gold mines. It hurt her to know she'd caused his flight, and she prayed he would find peace, as would her sister Olive. Olive continued to live in the shadow of grief, crawling through each day without words or hope. Although her sister's form was present downstairs, her spirit was still locked inside a prison of despair. Lilly knew only Christ held the keys to her freedom.

Bonnie buttoned up the dress in back while Lilly fiddled with the veil.

"You're beautiful," her mother said, and Lilly caught a glistening in her eye. "I'm so glad you waited for the Lord's choice."

Lilly nodded and bit her lip to keep her own eyes from filling.

Her sister and mother left her alone, then, to sort out her last moments. Lilly listened to shuffling below, then the sound of Willard, plunking out a hymn on the piano. The stairs creaked, and Lilly recognized the footfalls of her father. She pulled a calming breath and felt a wave of peace fill her just as a rap sounded on the door.

Lilly opened the door. Her father looked dapper in a black woolen suit. A smile creased his face, but tears in his eyes choked his voice. "This would be more difficult if Heinrick wasn't such a good man."

His words left her speechless, so she wound her arm through his and nodded.

Her father patted her hand and escorted her down the stairs. The parlor overflowed with guests, a smaller crowd than would have been at the church, but even so, a solid, well-wishing crew. At the end of the room, next to the fireplace, which glowed, waited Heinrick. He appeared every inch the hero she knew him to be. His blond hair was clipped short, but the curly locks refused to lie flat. She noticed his clean-shaven chin and the outline of thick muscles over his tailored navy blue suit. His job as brakeman on the Milwaukee Road and part-time hand on the Clark farm kept him in good shape and had cultivated in him an aura of confidence. He'd become a man who made others feel safe and comfortable.

Lilly's heart fluttered as Heinrick's blue eyes locked on hers. Then his mouth gaped in an open smile, and written on his face was a tangible delight. She wanted to sing. He was a hard man to unsettle, but obviously the sight of his bride had unraveled his stalwart composure. She floated toward Heinrick and the new preacher from Java, noting the happiness glinting in her mother's eyes and others who thought, a year earlier, Heinrick was the enemy.

Even Erica Torgesen was radiant, grinning uncontrollably in her new sky blue wool suit. Lilly slid her hand into Heinrick's gentle grip and felt embraced by the love shimmering in his eyes. In a trembling voice, Heinrick pledged to love and care for her as long as they lived. Then, he cradled her face between his wide hands and kissed her. At that moment, Lilly knew she would be forever thankful to God for bringing the enemy into her midst.

Rose gold sunshine flooded the room as they marched down the aisle. And, as Lilly glanced up at her young, handsome husband, she knew, one step at a time, she was walking in the fullness of joy.

A Letter To Our Readers

Dear Reader:

In order that we might better contribute to your reading enjoyment, we would appreciate your taking a few minutes to respond to the following questions. We welcome your comments and read each form and letter we receive. When completed, please return to the following:

Fiction Editor
Heartsong Presents
PO Box 719
Uhrichsville, Ohio 44683

1. Did you enjoy reading *Letters From the Enemy* by Susan May Warren?
   ❑ Very much! I would like to see more books by this author!
   ❑ Moderately. I would have enjoyed it more if

   _____

   _____

   _____

2. Are you a member of **Heartsong Presents**? ❑ Yes ❑ No
   If no, where did you purchase this book? _____

   _____

3. How would you rate, on a scale from 1 (poor) to 5 (superior), the cover design? _____

4. On a scale from 1 (poor) to 10 (superior), please rate the following elements.

   ____ Heroine   ____ Plot
   ____ Hero   ____ Inspirational theme
   ____ Setting   ____ Secondary characters

5. These characters were special because?_____

_____

_____

6. How has this book inspired your life?_____

_____

_____

7. What settings would you like to see covered in future
   Heartsong Presents books? _____

_____

_____

8. What are some inspirational themes you would like to see
   treated in future books? _____

_____

_____

9. Would you be interested in reading other **Heartsong
   Presents** titles? ❏ Yes   ❏ No

10. Please check your age range:
   ❏ Under 18   ❏ 18-24
   ❏ 25-34   ❏ 35-45
   ❏ 46-55   ❏ Over 55

Name_____

Occupation _____

Address _____

City_____ State_____ Zip_____

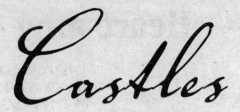

Castles

4 stories in 1

The "merrie old days" of the Middle Ages leave much to be desired for four women in England and France. None of them ever believed they'd be embroiled in such plots of devastation and danger. Can God rescue them from the emotional dungeons they face—and lower the drawbridges into the hearts of the men they love? Meet four memorable characters created by respected author Tracie Peterson, and see if they can turn cavernous medieval castles into heavenly havens.

Historical, paperback, 464 pages, 5 3/16"x 8"

❤ ❤ ❤ ❤ ❤ ❤ ❤ ❤ ❤ ❤ ❤ ❤ ❤ ❤ ❤ ❤

❤ ❤ ❤ ❤ ❤ ❤ ❤ ❤ ❤ ❤ ❤ ❤ ❤ ❤ ❤

Heart❤ong

Presents

Great Inspirational Romance at a Great Price!

Heartsong Presents books are inspirational romances in contemporary and historical settings, designed to give you an enjoyable, spirit-lifting reading experience. You can choose wonderfully written titles from some of today's best authors like Peggy Darty, Sally Laity, Tracie Peterson, Colleen L. Reece, Debra White Smith, and many others.

When ordering quantities less than twelve, above titles are $3.25 each.
Not all titles may be available at time of order.